"The stories in Seth Borgen's remarkable and compassionate collection deal with human relationships—quirky, sad, funny, heartbreaking—and the theme of love is the force that drives them along in often surprising ways. *If I Die in Ohio* is just the beginning of a long and brilliant career."

— DONALD RAY POLLOCK

author of *The Devil All the Time* and *Knockemstiff*

"These are the kind of heartbreaking, vulnerable tough-guy—and trying-to-be-tough guys, and the occasional trying-to-be-tough gals—stories we haven't seen the likes of in a long time. They made me think of Richard Yates, God rest his beautiful soul, and of Ray Carver. What does it mean to be a man, to be a husband, to be a father, to be *good*? Seth Borgen has a light hand with these heavy questions, and these stories brought me damn near close to tears too many times to count."

— MICHELLE HERMAN

author of *Devotion* and *Stories We Tell Ourselves*

"Whether walking the blistered streets of Tijuana, lying on an Ohio lakefront beach, or sipping champagne at a glittery Paris soirée, Borgen's sharp prose and pitch-perfect details will lead you through stories you never saw coming. Along the way you'll meet deeply flawed (but unflinchingly honest) characters you can't help but like, even as they make choices you would never recommend. *If I Die in Ohio* is so beautifully unexpected, brimming with lines you'll want to read again and again (and then again). Do yourself a favor, and let Borgen surprise you in all the best ways."

— ANNE CORBITT

author of the Nilsen Literary Prize recipient *Rules for Lying*

IF I DIE IN OHIO

stories

Seth Borgen

newamericanpress

Milwaukee, Wis.

newamericanpress

© 2019 by Seth Borgen

Printed in the United States of America

ISBN 9781941561171

Interior design by David Bowen

Cover design by Anneabel Gemmel
https://www.anneabelgemmel.com

For ordering information, please contact:
Ingram Book Group
One Ingram Blvd.
La Vergne, TN 37086
Phone: (800) 937-8000
Fax: (800) 876-0186
https://www.ingramcontent.com
orders@ingrambook.com

For event and media requests, please contact:
New American Press
www.newamericanpress.com
newamericanpress@gmail.com

To the investors.

More for their dedication and faith than their business acumen.

✶ ✶ ✶ ✶ ✶ ✶ CONTENTS ✶ ✶ ✶ ✶ ✶ ✶

"This is only denied to God: the power to undo the past."

— *Agathon, Athenian poet*

"Ray, when someone asks you if you're a god, you say, 'Yes'!"

— *Winston Zedemore, Ghostbuster*

ASTRO PIG

On his third marriage, the one he wouldn't survive, my father took me and his new family to the beach for a week. I was fifteen then. His new family was a stepdaughter, a stepson, both bony and secretive, and a wife, Pam, a lumpy-assed penny pincher who methodically cut her dinners in two and saved the other half for lunch the next day. She brought a purse full of coupons with her and we ate nothing but Subway the entire trip.

"Not this beach," I explained to my wife, Leigh, "but a beach."

She was pulling shirts and shorts from out of suitcases, folding and stacking them in the drawers of a cabinet. I examined the clock radio on the nightstand next to our bed and picked an individual grain of sand off my shoe.

"Are you going to fuck me at least once while we're here?" she said.

"Well," I said, "when you say it like that."

She called her two boys, Morgan, seven, and Claude, six, in from the beach. They stood just inside the open screen door, blue-lipped and dripping, facing the dark of the room, sun blasting behind them. Leigh stripped off their bathing suits and dried Morgan with a beach towel.

Morgan's hated me for several months and, standing there, grotesquely exposed, his mother shammying him in front of me must have been like death and I couldn't help but think Leigh knew that. Even if I did think of them as my boys and wasn't made uncomfortable by their nakedness, I would find this unsettling. Claude, though, didn't seem to notice he was naked. Rocking back and forth on the rounds of his feet, he could have been waiting for a train. Leigh sent Morgan to the shower, a pink blur in the corner of my eye, and put the towel to Claude. I refocused my attention back onto the clock radio.

"Look," Claude said. "It's like a joystick."

Leigh still toweling him off, I glanced up to Claude's tiny peter, pulsing hard and pointing at me.

"I wish your father knew what to do with one of those," Leigh said.

"Look, Dad," he said, smiling like a monkey, knocking his erection from side to side with his hips. "It's like a joystick."

Moments later, while Leigh was inside in the shower scrubbing the salt and sweat off Morgan and Claude, I stood out on the deck smoking a cigarette and asking myself what I was doing in this marriage. We were both twenty-nine, Leigh and I. I married her a year ago because she was elegant and graceful and I could imagine her in her forties looking like Juliet Binoche and me being the envy of the cocktail circuit because I'm the forty-ish guy who married a woman like that. She told Morgan and Claude to call me Dad and, when we were not fighting, told me to think of them as mine. But I didn't and hadn't slept with Leigh in three months.

"Juliet Binoche, my ass," I whispered, wondering where in the hell a cocktail circuit was.

I flicked my cigarette over the railing and the butt landed in a cluster of sand grass next to something dead. A guinea pig. I hopped the railing and knelt in the sand for a closer look. I had never seen a dead guinea pig. I had never seen a guinea pig that wasn't nibbling and twitching inside a translucent plastic cage that smelled of cedar and urine.

He was half-white, half the color of a new baseball mitt, his legs skyward, frozen in mid lunge, his black eyes wide and mouth gaped in an O as though he died seeing God. White string, tied around what I assumed was his waist, spooled away from the carcass and disappeared in the sand grass. Crabwalking, I followed the string about three feet to a deflated red balloon. I picked up the balloon and stretched it out. Written in black Sharpie were the words Astro Pig.

"Whatcha doing, Dan?" Claude stood on the deck behind me, his wet hair combed and parted like he belonged on a Christmas card.

"Dan?" I said.

"Mom just told us to call you Dan."

"Did she?"

"Yeah," he said.

"What do you think about that?"

"Dad. Dan," he said. "It's almost the same. Right?"

"Darn near," I said.

"So, watcha doing?"

"Why," I said, picking up Astro Pig by his string and holding him out to Claude like a ten-pound bass, "this is Astro Pig."

"Astro Pig?" he said.

"Astro Pig."

"Is he dead?"

"Oh, yeah," I said. "He's dead."

"Dead things are scary," he said, squinting, craning forward his neck to get a better look at the thing that was scary.

"Not this guy," I said. "He died a hero. He died reaching for the cosmos."

"Cosmos," repeated Claude. "Cosmos."

I asked Claude if he wanted to do something and he said that he did. We walked away from the bungalow, Astro Pig swinging to and fro from his string, me thinking about the trip to the beach when Pam and her kids were still called the new family. It's the fourth day that I really remember, me bobbing in the ocean, Pam and her son and daughter wading knee-deep, engaged in private talk. I heard yells for help and, about a football field out,

my father was thrashing and waving his arms. By the time I got to him he was barely swatting at the water, his eyes too lolled to focus. I pulled him in. Emerging from the foam and backwash,
his arm slung over my shoulders, he walked like a drunk man to our blankets and towels and collapsed.

I sat down next to him Indian style. With every few breaths he would choke on the air, but the rising and falling of his chest soon evened. Then, lying there, a calm overtook him. A calm like I'd never seen before. Like a man fresh out of mysteries.

"You know what I didn't do?" he said to me, his shaking hand reaching out for my knee.

"What?" I said.

"Try floating for a while." He said this and smiled. And then I smiled. His eyes, I don't think, needed to be open for him to know that it was just me. That the new family was still in the water and hadn't noticed a thing.

Claude beside me, we stepped out onto the almost empty beach, the setting sun sprawling the shadows of umbrellas and abandoned buckets ten, fifteen feet. I set down Astro Pig gently and flattened a patch of sand with my foot.

"Can you find me some rocks?" I said, holding out my fist. "About this big?"

"How many?"

"Just make a pile."

Claude made his pile and I gathered up dead grass, a McDonald's bag, some handbills advertising full-body massages, anything that would burn. I tore it all up and made a bed of tickertape in the center of the flattened patch.

"Do you need more?" asked Claude, dropping two chunks of asphalt onto his pile.

"No," I said. "You did great."

With the rocks, I made a circle around the bits of paper and grass. I lifted up Astro Pig by his string, laid him in the center, and shrouded him with his balloon.

"Do you know what a Viking funeral is?" I asked Claude.

"A funeral for Vikings?"

"It's a noble farewell to a noble soul."

I lit the paper in four places and stepped back. White smoke thinned out into the air, the orange fire hollow in what was left of the daylight. Crackling, then sizzling, the balloon blackened and twisted to reveal Astro Pig's fur smoldering into feathery golden rods.

"Viking funeral!" Claude shouted, running in a circle, kicking up sand. "Viking funeral! Viking funeral!"

Try floating for a while. When my father said that, I thought I knew what he meant. It didn't take me long to understand that I didn't. That night, to celebrate his new lease on life, we ate Subway again, Pam wrapping half of her sandwich in cellophane. As did my father, which I'd never seen him do before.

"Do we eat him now?" asked Claude, Astro Pig a black potato inside the dying fire.

"Do you want to eat him?" I asked.

He shrugged. I looked down at the top of his head, rested my hand on his shoulder and knew I would be the first person he hated. His world today was the size of four people and, in his mind, we're all happy. That won't last. Six more months, tops. Then this new hate will come crashing in on him like the head of a new poured Guinness. Because I don't make his mother happy. Because his dad, his real dad, is never coming back. I wanted to tell him that I was sorry.

"No, we're not going to eat him." We sat down together. I could smell the burning rubber, fur, paper, and grass all at the same time, each one distinctly. "We're going to leave him here. We're going to go out to dinner, come back, watch a movie and, tonight, while we're all asleep, the ocean is going to come up and carry Astro Pig away."

"Where's it gonna take him?"

"Valhalla," I said.

"What's Valhalla?"

"It's like heaven, but better."

"And that's what you get when you die reaching for the cosmos?"

"You better fucking believe it, Claudy."

He thought about this, then nodded. "That sounds good," he said.

I sometimes get the sense that Morgan and Claude's dad saw all of this coming. When he figured out what it was that he had with Leigh, that it was no way to live, and that it was going to take getting the hell out of there to find a way that was, that's exactly what he did. And if he'd stuck around and if he had seen what Leigh pulled back in the bungalow, using Claude like that, maybe he would have killed her. What he wouldn't have done was stand there like an idiot, go out onto the deck for a cigarette, and then spend the rest of his life with this woman.

"Dan," said Claude, "are you going to leave us?"

"Why would you think that?" I said.

"Morgan said you are."

"When did he say that?"

"All the time."

I wasn't. Some men just don't have that in them. Leaving. Even when it's the right thing to do. Not my dad, no matter what he thought while in the fist of that current, shouting for help, staggering back to his blanket, using his son like a cane, imagining all of the ways his life was going to be different from that moment on. I wish I had told him that I knew he didn't want to die alone and that a marriage was a lonely place to be when that's all you wanted from it. But I didn't know that then.

"No, Claude," I said. "I'm not going anywhere."

"When you die," he said, "are you going to have a Viking funeral? Like Astro Pig?"

"Well, I'd have to become a Viking first," I said. "Wouldn't I?"

He agreed that was true. I mussed his damp hair and, right then, I didn't just like Claude. Liking him was always easy. I loved him. I loved him because he was not my son and because he never would be. He was the son of a man who had the guts to walk away from bad love. And for that, for Claude, I was grateful.

BATHING SUIT PARTS

ONE AFTERNOON IN 1958, THE SUMMER AFTER I GRADUATED from Barberton High, my girlfriend Kaye and I drove downtown to Lake Anna, parked in front of Soames Handmade Furniture, and walked in our bathing suits across the street and down the grassy incline towards the brown water. We swam a bit, left the boys and the few girls to their laughing and splashing, bought a small box of popcorn at the concession stand in the bathhouse, and set our blanket out on the grass. A man nearby whose face looked made of brick watched us over the curve of his fat wife as we stretched out, families chattering all around, to let the sun dry us.

Sleepy, my mind drifted in and around the realities of never running track again, leaving Barberton, Ohio for college, whether I wanted to spend the rest of my life with Kaye knowing I didn't but knowing also I wanted to have sex before I left.

After some time, I felt Kaye sit up. "Harry," she said. "There's something going on over there."

"Over where?" I said, tilting my head skyward and seeing red through my closed eyelids.

"Over there," she said, but I knew where she meant. The roped off area on the far side of Lake Anna where the black folks swam.

"The Black Sea?" I said, and smiled.

"You shouldn't call it that."

"I didn't name it," I said, leaning up and opening my eyes. All I could see was sharp light glinting off water and wet bodies.

"Of course not," she said, her eyes focused across the lake. "No one starts a thing like that. They just, what's the word, perpetuate it."

"OK, OK. What is it?"

She pointed, but that didn't help. I squinted, sharpened my sight, and when my eyes adjusted, there was a crowd of blacks in bathing suits standing at their water's edge, some of them yelling. All of the black swimmers were either out of the water or almost out.

"Probably a fight," I said and dug into the popcorn, crunched, and wiped my oily fingers on my trunks. Kaye's body and eyes were fixed. "It's a fight," I said again. "Have some popcorn."

I leaned back on my elbows and tugged on Kaye's shoulder, as if to physically pull her back into our warm dreaminess. She wore her two-piece, the one with the bottoms that hung sexy and low on her hips. The Black Sea held her attention for a moment and she turned to me slowly.

"I don't want any more popcorn," she said.

"Yeah," I said. The popcorn was burned, the yellow and black looking as though we were sharing a swarm of bees. "It's not great."

We had been steady for over a year and I'd not yet seen more of her body than I could see in her two-piece. There was the several second feel the night we lost at States and I had to act like that was some favor. We made out in my Nash most every Friday and Saturday and each time she'd tell me not to touch her "bathing suit parts."

"But those are the best parts," I'd say, and she'd tell me that wasn't funny. I wouldn't tell her I wasn't trying to be funny.

I'd rolled the bones on young Miss Kaye Sagemiller with a hunch there was something in her less prim than I was supposed to think. She was the kind of pretty I thought worth the gamble. My friends aimed a little lower and, thirteen months later, were telling stories of buttery warmths and coming so hard they could feel it in their colons and that I should, "Hang in there."

She still wasn't totally with me and this was happening more and more. She would sometimes get bighearted and I couldn't tell if it was real or show. We once saw a middle-aged man eating alone in a restaurant. Kaye leaned across the table and whispered, "I want to cry." I asked her about it later in the night and she didn't remember saying it.

I tugged on her shoulder again and something in her lightened. She closed her eyes and smiled, her nose shiny and red from the sun. She nudged my bicep with her forehead and she was with me again.

We both lay down, her head resting on my shoulder. I was near asleep and thinking about *Huckleberry Finn*. I read it in English class that year but I wasn't thinking about the book as it was but how I had envisioned the book growing up. Barefoot children running through green meadows and languid rivers gently carrying small boats anywhere. The book itself was boring and there were too many characters and I was happier having forgotten most of it.

Kaye leaned up again and shook me. "Harry," she said. "Look."

An ambulance sat on the Black Sea's grassy incline, its light spinning, surrounded by black folks pointing towards the water.

"Just like a nigger to bring a razor to a picnic," said the man with the face made of brick.

"What happened?" said Kaye.

I think I said, "I'm sure it's nothing," but I may not have. The white children on our side were splashing and shooting through the water like penguins. "No fair! No fair!" some boy shouted amidst some game. "Is too fair!" shouted another. The water on the far side was empty.

I knew Kaye was going to tell me to go over there and I was thinking of reasons not to when she did. White people did not go to the Black Sea in the summertime. The World War I cannon children played on, the World War II memorial, the gazebo, the concession stand and the bathhouse were all on our side. I had walked the sidewalk rimming Lake Anna many times, many times with Kaye, but never in the summer.

But these were not good reasons. They were not reasons at all. Whatever they were, they cycled through my mind as I stood, walked slow to the sidewalk, hoping others would join me, and the only reason that stuck was that if this mattered to Kaye and I did nothing, what a waste those thirteen months would have been.

No one else joined me.

The energy at the Black Sea was heavy and terrible and I went entirely unnoticed. I didn't talk to anyone and no one talked to me, but there was talk all around. A girl had drowned. Her mother sat in the grass clutching a towel to her mouth, staring at the water. She looked helpless and naked in her light purple bathing suit.

One paramedic leaned against the ambulance while the other said to nine or ten black men that they couldn't do anything without a body. I looked at the water and was sure every twig and every leaf and every candy bar wrapper was the surfacing of something dead.

All of the men and the boys deemed old enough waded out into the water and formed a human chain. I saw myself through Kaye's eyes, standing there, awkward and useless. "We need more men!" someone in the chain shouted. Some black teenagers walked around me, towards the water, and I walked with them. We linked arms, one of the teenagers to my left, one of the men who spoke to the paramedics to my right, and moved forward in unison.

We combed the water with our bodies, from shallow to deep. No one in the chain spoke. Their faces were tight with knotted jawbones. Being there did not feel good or right, and terror pulled at my skin from the inside when algae brushed my leg or I stepped on a rock. My heart was a fist. I looked back at the beach. Both paramedics were leaning against the ambulance. Some policemen held their arms out and casually said, "Remain calm. Remain calm." Every woman and child was frozen, watching us.

"So is Kaye," I said to myself. "So is Kaye. So is Kaye."

I was in stomach deep when the girl's suit, empty as a windsock, the same purple as the mother's, appeared in the water in front of me. The chain broke not far from me to my right. A man lifted the girl from the water, holding her as though she were delicate. She was nine, ten, or eleven, bony weight in the man's arms, her eyes lolled back, her lips and nipples the same black-purple.

I picked her suit out of the water and held it towards the man next to me. "This is hers," I said, but he didn't hear me or care. "This is hers," I said to the teenagers and they didn't look at me either.

The chain converged on the girl and they all seemed to carry her as one. I walked away from them, alone towards shore, the water holding me like gravity.

I walked the sidewalk fast. I cut my heel on a sharp stone and kept moving. I imagined telling Kaye, "If you care about the niggers so damn much why didn't you go?" and didn't know why I thought that. As I got closer, I wanted childish things. To cry. To be held. To come around the arc of Lake Anna, see my blanket, my girl, her fingers wrung with worry, her big, soft blue eyes pulling me in.

When I got to the grassy incline, when I found my blanket, Kaye lay asleep, her eyes shielded from the sun by the inside of her elbow. I stood there. I'll never know how long. The white children played in their water. Their parents watched or chatted with one another. The man whose face was made of brick ate an egg-salad sandwich and said something to his fat wife about their lawn. A line swirled from the concession stand. Across the lake, the dead girl was sliding into the ambulance on a gurney, her bathing suit still in my hand, and there wasn't a goddamn thing on Earth I wanted to look at.

PROVO FOR GOOD

PIN CHRISTIANSON AND JOHNNA GREW UP TOGETHER. THEY LOOKED like sisters. THEY graduated high school the same year, loaded up one car, and moved to Provo to attend Brigham Young. They were both married at twenty-three. It wasn't until Pin's husband started bloodying her face that their paths finally split. Much to Johnna's relief, Pin always suspected. A permanent upper hand that went without saying. They were both twenty-five.

Pin left Provo once the divorce was final and went home to live with her parents. If her parents were aware of this fact, they kept that awareness to themselves. She was there for six months when she wanted to see if she could choke herself to death with her own hands. She assumed she'd fail at that, too and did. Iridescent pinpricks whirled within her eyes before she removed her thumbs from her throat and dialed Johnna's number.

"Could I come stay with you and Lucas for a short while?" she asked.

"You sound hoarse," said Johnna.

"I'm just a little sick."

Back in Provo, Johnna and Lucas's living room was the same and they were all the same in it. Pin on the far end of an orange couch. Lucas on the floor playing a speedboat videogame. Johnna in a green chair sliding her Polaroids of Beijing fire escapes into tiny thrift store frames. Since her arrival, they'd asked several different ways if she was planning on returning to Provo for good. She told them she was weighing her options. She had no other options. It just seemed like the right thing to say.

Johnna and Lucas were her good friends. But they knew they were her good friends. And they knew they were her only friends. They were equals once. Now she felt as serious and whole to them as a favored pet. Pin was sitting there, her hands folded neatly in her lap, wondering what their faces would do if their pet suddenly picked up one of Johnna's frames, shattered it against the wall, grabbed Lucas's video game system—its wires dragging like a dead squid's tentacles—and tossed it straight out the window when Johnna said something to Lucas about a peacock.

"I'm sorry," said Pin. "What about a peacock?"

"Lucas's friend," Johnna said. "Ned Peacock. He'll be staying with us for a few days."

Pin watched Johnna talk more than she heard the words. She was watching what made people say, "You two could be twins." Dark eyes and dark hair and similar skins pulled over similar skulls. But even between identical twins there was a pretty one. Johnna had a lightness about her, one that came from someplace deep down and gave her face this extra something. Because people don't mention things like that, Pin had no idea when Johnna developed this. Or when Pin lost hers. Or if she ever had it.

"Oh?"

"Oh, indeed," Lucas said to the television screen. "He'll be here within the hour."

"Did I know this and forget?"

"We just found out today."

"Oooh, we should get sushi," said Johnna, her hands gliding over the chipped and dusty frames. "Does Ned eat sushi?"

"Everyone eats sushi."

"You both sound so excited."

"I'm a lot excited. We grew up together. He's very clever."

"He is very clever," agreed Johnna, intensely emphasizing the is. "I would describe him as being an exciting young man."

"This all seems awfully convenient," said Pin. "You guys aren't trying to set the two of us up, are you?" She meant this as a joke, funny because, surely, out of respect for what she's been through, it would be too soon for something like that.

That's not how Johnna took it. Her face became grave. She reached out to Pin and squeezed her hand. "Oh, no, sweetie," she said, as if were explaining something to a horse. "He's not Mormon."

When she was certain that notion was out of Pin's little head, Johnna went back to her Beijing fire escapes. Many of the old frames contained old pictures. Drawings and photos of strangers taken by strangers. The ones she had already removed lay stacked at her feet. A Mexican woman standing in front of a propane tank. A charcoal etching of Waylon Jennings.

Pin sat quietly and refolded her hands in her lap. Right out the window, she thought, staring at Lucas's video game system.

Johnna and Lucas lived on the second floor of a Victorian house long ago split in half and converted into two apartments. After the knock at the door, after Lucas paused his game and exploded down the stairs like a child, after Johnna clapped her hands lightly and said, "Ned's here," Lucas escorted the unfamiliar boy up the stairs and into the living room.

Johnna rose to her feet and kissed Ned's cheek, and Lucas threw an arm around his neck. They spoke in the code of old friends. Inside jokes and half-sentences, all of it sounding to Pin like some language twins used. None of it seemed particularly clever to her. The folded hands in her lap were sweating, but she didn't know what else to do with them.

"You look awful," said Lucas. "You look like you've spent ten hours in a car."

"I've been driving for days. I'm sure I look like a sack of garbage."

"Lucas. You're terrible. Ned does not look awful." Johnna said, over-pronouncing each syllable. "He looks fantastic. Pin, tell Ned he looks fantastic."

She studied him. His brown, low-top Chuck Taylors with no socks. Corduroys rolled above the ankle. A light blue high school girl's softball T-shirt with orange lettering that was plastered to his torso with sweat. He was delicate in the face with small shoulders. Pin thought him more pretty than handsome.

"Fantastic," she said.

Ned looked at her and smiled. And it wasn't a Provo smile, either. It had been a year since she had gotten any other kind. The self-righteously sympathetic kind that hung on the faces of the nosey and meddlesome, which in Provo was everyone. Lucas and Johnna went on with their fawning, Johnna saying how funny Ned's shirt was and Lucas saying that he's been wearing that same shirt since he was fifteen. While all this was going on, Ned went right on giving her that smile. Pin had been alive long enough to know what was going on. She was being sized up.

"And this is our Pin," said Johnna. "She's my very best friend. She's visiting us, too."

Ned held out his hand to her. She unfolded her fingers and took it. It was sweaty as hers.

"Steering wheel," he said.

"Submissive posture," she said.

He sat next to her, close to her, on the orange couch. Johnna went back to her green chair and Lucas to the floor, his back to the paused videogame. Once they were settled, Ned finally looked away from Pin and to Lucas. Then to Johnna.

"What's for dinner?" he said. "I passed a sushi place down the street. Do you guys eat sushi?"

Almost everyone Pin knew was Mormon. And almost all of them smelled exactly the same. Like how Adam—her ex-husband—always smelled. Dryer sheets and baby powder. Ned smelled like a body. Like skin and sweat.

"Everyone eats sushi," said Pin.

Pin had, for the most part, avoided setting foot outside Johnna and Lucas's apartment, not wanting to see Adam. He still lived in Provo, somewhere, and was engaged again. To a girl Pin once considered a friend. But she wasn't thinking about any of that, walking the two blocks to the restaurant. The air felt good on her body and it felt good to breathe. The sky was blue and the purple Rockies cradled the quiet city and she walked side-by-side with Johnna, Lucas and Ned walking side-by-side a few steps ahead. The low-hanging sun stretched their shadows across the passing lawns and Pin thought, Yes, make all the people disappear and Provo really was a lovely place.

"I love how much Lucas loves his old friends," Johnna whispered. "Of all of them, Ned's my favorite."

"He's very nice."

"He is." Johnna cupped her mouth with her hand and whispered even softer, "But he sometimes swears."

There was a bounce to the way Ned and Lucas walked together. It was easy to imagine them twelve, thirteen—the years right before things start getting hard and never stop—cutting through neighbors' yards back in their hometown beneath canopies of swaying leaves. They never grew up and the world was okay with that. It had pulled them aside when they were boys and told them the last thing it would ever need was two more men.

"Please don't tell him I'm divorced," Pin whispered back.

Johnna took her hand and leaned her head on Pin's shoulder. Pin closed her eyes and pretended, for a moment, that they were all children. She wanted to play in a garden and someone to tell her secrets to.

And secrets. She wanted some of those, too.

The restaurant was quiet and dark, lit only by small votive candles inside glass orbs at the center of each table. Pin sat across from Ned, Johnna across from Lucas and, soon, the table was covered with California rolls and spider rolls and cucumber rolls and Philly rolls and eel and fried vegetables. It was common for Lucas and Johnna to drift off and spend entire meals lost within their own little married world. When they began holding hands across the table, Pin knew that's where they were. She and Ned could burst into flames and it might take a while for their friends to notice.

"Do you take for granted how healthy and attractive Mormons are?" asked Ned, mixing soy sauce and wasabi. "It's like you were all raised on milk and apples."

"They make all kinds of us these days," she said. "Healthy, attractive, ugly, mean, stupid."

"Yeah, yeah. And there's no Great Pumpkin." He smiled with only half his mouth. "Humor me, I'm on vacation." He raised one hand as if making an edict. "All Mormons are healthy and attractive."

Pin had heard stories. From where, she couldn't say. Stories about young men who fetishized LDS girls. Young men, Methodists maybe, who'd heard stories themselves about how LDS girls were raised to use the less-than-permanent sexual activities on convertible males and the world-curious LDS boys during their hormonal years to keep them in the flock. If there were truth to this, it meant Pin was raised wrong. She wasn't ruling that out. Nor was she ruling out that Ned Peacock had heard these same stories. It would certainly explain a human being vacationing in Provo, Utah if he could help it.

"Is that why you're here? For healthy, attractive Mormons?"

"I'm here to see them," he said, motioning to Johnna and Lucas with his head. "Though they are healthy and attractive."

"They are." Pin tried to strike a balance between eating and talk, but everything she put into her mouth was a waste of time. Talk was what she wanted. "What do you know about Mormons, besides the things you only think you know?"

"That's an interesting question."

"Thank you."

Ned darted his eyes in Lucas and Johnna's direction. He was about to tell her something. Something he didn't want Johnna and Lucas in on. She snuck a look at them out of the sides of her eyes and they were still a thousand miles away. She and Ned leaned in close to one another, the candlelight tangling lip and nose shadows upward on their faces.

"I once asked Lucas about the," Ned pretended to cough so that he could hide his mouth with his fist, "temple garments."

"Oh, yeah? And what did he say?"

"Something to the effect of them being an antiquated, long-abandoned custom and that stories of their use today are, by and large, myths."

"And you were not satisfied with that answer?"

"You probably don't need me telling you this, but there's this thing—" Ned pointed to Lucas with his eyebrow rather than saying his name, "—does when he's not being one-hundred percent truthful."

"What's that?"

"He lies through his ever-loving teeth."

"Yes," Pin said. "It's a subtle tell."

Oh, no, sweetie. She heard Michele's voice in her head. *He's not Mormon.* What did she know? What did either of them know other than how to be like them? She was doing just fine and, in any event, if they were such good judges of character, how'd they miss the way he had looked at her, was still looking at her? Or the way she'd been looking at him? Or what was palpably happening just inches from their healthy, attractive, oblivious elbows?

"So what is the deal with them?" he said, completely ignoring his food. "The, you know, garments. Or do I not want to know?"

"Some say once you're a good, married Mormon, you wear them no matter what. And some don't say that. It depends on how much being in good standing with the church means to you."

"How's their standing?" He again pointed to Johnna and Lucas with his eyebrow.

"Unimpeachable."

He nodded. "And how's yours?"

"Mine?"

He nodded again.

They were no longer talking about temple garments. They were talking about the intimacy of discarded objects drifting through space, their paths crossing every now and then for blinks of time. But in those blinks they share the same cold, the same dark, the same weight and weightlessness. The same endless forever until the pull of some new planet reels them in. But gravity cares only about where an object is going.

"It depends on the day."

So what if he had heard stories about promiscuous Mormon girls. Right then, she had trouble seeing anything wrong with that. And if there was a sin somewhere in there, she couldn't see that either. Maybe some young LDS girls relieving a young Adam of some of his pressures earlier in life would have saved a lot of people a lot of trouble.

Back at the house, Lucas and Ned sat on the living room floor, sifting through a cardboard box Lucas kept under his bed filled with photographs, yearbooks, notes—every scrap of paper he still had from middle school and high school. Pin and Johnna sat on the orange couch, drinking tea, laughing and listening to fifteen years' worth of stories.

"Most of the time, I have no idea who they're talking about," said Johnna, "but I can't help but laugh."

During her first semester at Brigham Young, Pin had a crush on Lucas. Most girls did. He had a nostalgia for his own childhood so thick it was like a force field between himself and what the world was really like. To be near him, you were safe, too, within his force field. He hosted Nintendo parties and movie nights where he showed The Karate Kid three times. He scoured thrift stores for the clothes he wore in middle school. Then everyone they knew started doing the same thing. Amid all of this, he fell in love with Johnna and not her. That seemed like a thousand years ago now.

"They really must have had a nice childhood," said Pin, sipping her tea, watching Ned's face turn red from laughter.

Adam was a friend of a friend and he was sometimes a part of that bubble they lived in during those years and sometimes he wasn't. Pin knew little about him. He asked her to marry him three times. The first two times, Johnna and Lucas were not yet engaged. The third time, they were. As was most everyone she knew. Alone started to feel like lonely. Lonely started to feel like alien. The third time, she considered it.

She called her mother and asked her what she should do. Her mother asked Pin what Adam was studying. "Law," Pin told her, and this pleased her mother. She asked Johnna, and Johnna told her to pray. So she did. She prayed to God for wisdom. She kneeled on the floor of her dorm room for hours, her fingers folded tight, listening into the silence for something. She pictured herself standing next to Adam in a photograph. How Adam was lanky and blonde, like Lucas. How they could be brothers just as her and Michele could be sisters. That they would make such similar couples soothed Pin and she mistook this for wisdom.

She grew up doing as she was supposed to and so did Adam and they were each other's first everything. None of it was very good. Most of it was worse. Maybe a decade of teenage celibacy had jarred something loose in Adam's brain and maybe that's why his ejaculations crippled him with shame. And why he was ashamed for wanting them in the first place. He would take her by the arm at the strangest times—as she was leaving the bathroom or separating the recycling—and, without looking at her, lead her towards the bedroom stammering "I need, I need—" Though Adam never could quite articulate what it was he needed, that meant sex. Sex that seemed to Pin more like the board game *Operation* than it did sex. Afterwards, he would cry and jerk away from her if she tried to touch him. It wasn't over until he found a reason to beat her with his fists sometime the next day. Always over nothing. Always methodical, again taking her by the arm, lifting his other arm above his head, pausing as if to take aim. And then a crack of light inside her

eyeballs. Lift, pause, crack. Lift, pause, crack. Straight-faced, too. No anger.
Just necessary force. Like hammering a nail.

Hammering a nail, Pin thought. Funny.

The room burst with white light as Johnna took a Polaroid of Lucas and
Ned. They went on with their stories, unaware they were participating in an
immortalized moment.

"Beth Tylicki was so attractive in middle school and became such a frump
in high school." Ned was flipping through a yearbook. "And Hillary Jacob was
such a frump in middle school and became so meow in high school."

"I'm not entirely convinced they didn't just trade names the summer
before freshman year."

"Whatever happened to them?"

"I think they're both married."

"Fuck," said Ned as if he'd just been told both girls died in separate plane
crashes. Lucas punched him in the forearm.

"Ned," Johnna gasped.

"Sorry, sorry," said Ned. "I forgot. I spent three years of my life swearing
in front of Lucas and getting punched in the arm before I finally figured out
the connection."

The word charged Pin's blood like adrenaline. No one in her sphere said
that word, especially within Lucas and Johnna's force field. The F-word. She
couldn't even formulate the word in her mind, yet Ned had smuggled it in
with him and there it was, filling the room. Pin wanted to press her body
against it.

"Say it again," she said.

"Fuck," he said and, again, Johnna gasped.

"Ned. Pin," she said. "Lucas. Punch Ned's arm again."

"Oh," said Lucas. "It's fine."

"Lucas!"

"No, no," said Ned. "I deserve it. Here." Ned held out his arm and lifted his
sleeve.

Lucas just barely punched his arm because, really, he was just barely offended. Johnna was maybe a little bit more offended, but they both knew their dreamy bubble would prevail, like always, and the room would be all light and warm and buzzing with peaceful joy again in a few moments. Pin wanted them to leave so that she could wrap Ned around her like a blanket and make him say "Fuck, fuck, fuck, fuck, fuck, fuck," until it was a different day outside. He was looking directly at her when he said "Fuck," one more time.

Around midnight, Lucas and Ned began repeating their stories, and Johnna's eyelids hung heavy like a lounging cat's. She got up and took her and Pin's teacups and saucers to the kitchen. Pin's bladder was full of tea. Afraid she might miss something, she had not once left the room.

"So, where am I sleeping?" asked Ned.

"We keep a bed in the attic." Lucas set the lid back on the memory box. "It's my favorite room in the house, but Johnna thinks it's spooky."

"I've been sleeping in my car on top of my possessions like a dragon since Kansas. I can handle spooky."

"What were you doing in Kansas?"

"I stopped at a replica of Dorothy Gale's house from *The Wizard of Oz*."

"What was that like?"

"The whole time I kept thinking, 'Toto, we are totally in Kansas right now.'"

Lucas took some sheets and blankets from his bedroom and opened the door leading up to the attic. Pin and Ned were alone in the living room. She stood, stretched her legs, and leaned her back against the wall. Ned got off the floor and walked to her. She thought the only reason he'd be coming towards her was because he wanted to lean against the wall where she was and tried to get out of his way. He put his hand on her left breast and set his chin on her shoulder.

"You shouldn't do that," Pin whispered.

"Why not?"

She didn't know why not.

They were on opposite sides of the living room when Lucas and Johnna reentered. Pin was still pressed against the wall. They each exchanged polite goodnights. Johnna hugged Ned and he disappeared up the attic stairs. She and Lucas walked hand-in-hand into their bedroom, and Pin could still feel the ghost of Ned Peacock's hand on her body.

A good Mormon woman was once a good Mormon girl who married a good Mormon boy in a temple. She wears temple garments under her clothes and will for the rest of her good Mormon life. There is a top piece and a bottom piece. They are the color of clean bones and look old even when they're new. Except for a crescent of neck, they cover from just above the knee to the shoulders, a symbolic armor against the evils of the world. As a subject of conversation, they are to be avoided. So, two years ago, when they began to sit on her skin like wool on rug burn, who was Pin supposed to talk to about that? Her mother? Johnna?

She removed her clothes and sat in the dark on the edge of her bed wearing only the temple garments. Faint light glowed underneath her door from Lucas and Johnna's room. They were praying. Pin couldn't remember the last time she prayed. After a half hour, the light went out. An hour later, the house was thick with silence.

She set out a new pair of underwear and a T-shirt on the bed. She looked at herself in the mirror, her white skin glowing blue in the moonshine. The girl in the mirror removed the temple garments. Standing there, her face unclear, she was nothing but soft curves floating in the blackness and couldn't remember ever being naked like this before. She hardly knew her body away from bathrooms or x-ray machines, away from white and metal rooms lit by cold, invasive lights.

She put on the new underwear. They were boy-cut and sat low on her hips. Then the T-shirt, which just barely covered the bumps of her hip bones. She knew well what sacred felt like and knew this was something else. Pin felt uncontained. Her body wanted to laugh from a place so deep down inside that it would never make it to her mouth.

She slipped out her door, floorboards creaking underneath the pads of her feet. Her breathing was shallow as she made her way up the stairs, into the attic. The air was heavy with dark and dust. A large round top window hung above the head of the bed and she walked towards its subtle, blue glow. Ned's eyes were open, watching her. Pin pictured what he saw. This slim, white ghost coming to him.

Pin straddled his stomach. Ned leaned up and the silhouette of his head, neck, and bare shoulders were black against the faint light outside. The round top window looked like a pair of wings growing from his back. She felt his hands on her hips. They moved upward, underneath her t-shirt, drumming over her ribs.

Because there's always time, if not much, between knowing that you are going to drown and when you finally stop kicking your legs, she whispered, "Don't take my underwear off."

One of his hands stayed within her T-shirt. The other slid into her underwear. Pin held onto his shoulders and leaned forward, pressing her forehead against the cool glass of the window. Choking on her own air, her eyes closed tight, she wanted Adam to see this. She wanted her parents to see this. She wanted God to see this. She opened her eyes and there was only an empty street. A swaying willow tree. The moon.

The next morning, Lucas and Ned went to an arcade to beat a videogame called *Golden Axe* "at least four times," according to Lucas. "At least," said Ned.

Pin, wearing her temple garments again underneath a white blouse, a thin maroon cardigan and a brown skirt, walked with Johnna to the farmer's market. Baskets of fresh berries and hand fruit sat out on metal folding tables underneath giant yellow umbrellas. Old men and old women whose skin looked made of leather manned the tables and haggled with faces familiar to Pin from church and school. She wasn't sure what to do with it all. These vibrant colors and these people. They knew her, or of her, because everyone knows everything about people like her, but today she didn't feel obligated to slouch her shoulders or avert her gaze to make it easier for them to judge or pity her. She knew something about herself that they couldn't possibly know, and this made Pin feel powerful.

"Jesus Christ was murdered by a riotous mob," said Pin.

Johnna held an orange in each hand, squeezing them for ripeness. "What?" she said over her shoulder.

"Jesus Christ was murdered by a riotous mob and sealed in a tomb."

"Yes, I suppose he was."

"When he rose from his tomb, what do you think he did first?"

Johnna paid for six oranges and tumbled them into the canvas tote hanging from her elbow. "I've never thought about it," she said.

They meandered to the next table. A dozen or so pomegranates, red and glossy and the size of human hearts, sat atop a blue blanket.

"Do."

"I don't know," said Johnna. "Pray?"

Pin held one of the pomegranates, pressing her thumb into its rubbery flesh. She had the urge to rip it open, like a savage, and squeeze a fistful of arils into her mouth. "I bet he was thirsty," she said.

Johnna tugged gently at the arm of Pin's sweater. Pin set the pomegranate back on the blue blanket and they moved on.

"Ned leaves tomorrow," said Johnna, and Pin wondered why she said that. If she knew more than she was letting on. Pin decided that there was no way she could and it wouldn't matter if she did.

"Is Lucas sad?"

"He is," Johnna said. "Ned's been a nice distraction, but Lucas has much to get back to."

"Like school."

"Yes."

"The church."

"Yes."

"You."

"Yes," said Johnna, who seemed to be barely paying attention. "Me."

A question formed in Pin's mind. One she knew she'd never ask. If Johnna enjoyed sex. Not necessarily with Lucas, but the act itself. If she didn't love him, would or could the physical connecting of two human bodies be enough for her? What if something were to happen to Lucas? What if people change? What made her so sure she was never going to wonder what it might be like with someone else?

She wasn't going to ask because she knew Johnna would answer without thinking and what the answer would be.

"These things are still there for you," Johnna said.

"What things?"

"School. The church." Johnna slid her arm gently inside Pin's. "Me."

Looking at Johnna was like looking at stupid, happy version of herself. In love because she didn't know any better and would never know better. About the world beyond being lucky enough to marry a boy who obliviously manufactured a pure and glowing goodness from his pure and glowing heart. Pin took Johnna's hand and pitied her.

"I bet he was thirsty," Pin repeated.

"I say he would have prayed."

That night, the four of them placed an order for two large vegetarian pizzas. Lucas asked Johnna if she'd mind going out alone to pick them up. When she was gone, Pin wondered what was strange about the three of them in that room together. Something was, to be sure, and it occurred to her finally. Everything changed when Johnna was someplace else.

Pin had never seen a joint before in real life but knew immediately what it was. Ned carried them in his pocket in a black tin shaped like a coffin. He was sitting next to her on the couch when he cracked open and closed the tin and produced the mummified cylinder to a marble-silent room. Lucas made a show of looking conflicted, chewing on his lower lip and rolling his eyes in thought.

"Right," said Ned. "Like this isn't why you sent Johnna for the pizzas."

Lucas smiled bigger than Pin had ever seen. He got up, spun Elton John's "Rocket Man" on his turntable, opened the window, and sat on the sill. Ned held the joint up to Pin. The gesture itself was a question. *When I really do hand this to you, will you take it?* Pin nodded her head yes.

Lucas knew what he was doing, lighting and exhaling outside the open window. Ned really knew what he was doing, his movements as clipped and matter-of-fact as a croupier. He handed her the joint and lighter and she lit it, inhaling and holding in what seemed to be only the taste of butane, like she was sucking on hot, dirty nickels. She passed it back to Ned and it moved between them enough times that she lost count. Pin did not know how much to take in, how long to hold it, if she was doing any of it right, what it would feel like when it started to work or even if it would work. She'd heard that sometimes it didn't take the first time.

"Rocket Man" wound to a finish and Lucas played it again, mouthing the words with his eyes closed during the slow parts, shaking his hair and slapping his knees in-time during the fast. In the middle of the third listen, or maybe the fourth, he sat bolt upright and grabbed Ned by the shoulder. "I can't believe I forgot," he said. "You'll never guess what I found." He jumped from the sill and ran to his and Johnna's bedroom. There was the clatter of rummaging followed by a muffled, drawn out, "Yesssss."

"This could be anything," said Ned. "Two-to-one says it's Teenage Mutant Ninja Turtles-related."

"Maybe he found where Johnna keeps his spine," she said, trying to remember how long it took to pick up two vegetarian pizzas.

"He wanted to be the fifth Ninja Turtle. Did you know that? Rembrandt. And his weapon was going to be some sort of a ninja whip."

Lucas returned to the room and his sill carrying a red spiral notebook.

It was ragged—its once sharp corners worn soft and round—with a strip of masking tape angled across the front. Written on the tape in black magic marker were the words *Great Big Ideas, Inc.*

"Oh, man," said Ned.

"When we were in middle school, Ned and I had the rest of our lives totally figured out." Lucas displayed for her the notebook. "Perhaps you didn't realize that you were in the same room as the cofounders of Great Big Ideas, Inc."

"We didn't even know what Inc. meant," said Ned.

"Tell me. What was Great Big Ideas, Inc.?"

"Only the best idea we've ever had," said Lucas. "A million of the best ideas we've ever had."

Ned turned towards Pin and his forehead was almost touching her shoulder. "That was our video game company."

"Who would know better what kind of games kids wanted to play than kids? The plan was to write down every video game idea we had growing up and then make and sell them when we were grown up," Lucas said. "That was our Great Big Idea."

"Shit, man," said Ned. "We're grown up."

"When was this dream abandoned?" She said this to both of them but was staring at the top of Ned's head.

"Are you kidding? It's full steam ahead now that we've unearthed phase one of our two-phase plan. Right partner?" Lucas smacked the notebook with the back of his hand. "I mean, we've got the ideas."

"All that's left is to learn how to make video games." Ned passed the joint to Lucas. He took it and seemed to immediately forget that it was in his hand.

"Pure gold. Listen, listen." Lucas crossed his legs and began reading over Elton John. "*Captain Fireballer.* A guy in the future travels to a bunch of different planets to fight alien armies. He can turn himself into a ball of fire that basically looks like a comet and fly really fast across the board like Sonic the Hedgehog, and every time he touches an alien like this the alien dies, but he can't do this for a very long at a time.'"

Ned kissed her shoulder. She could hear his lips more than she could feel them. Through cardigan, blouse, and temple garment, it was barely the warmth of his breath that she felt. This warmth, though, turned kinetic inside her and poured outward through her neurons, then back, then out again, like water sloshing in a bathtub.

"'When he isn't a flying fireball, he fights the aliens with Wolverine claws but only on one hand and two claws instead of three. Costume will be blue with a helmet that looks like a *Robotech* helmet.'"

His mouth moved from shoulder to the skin of her neck. These she could feel. These she could really feel. He slid his hand underneath and up her blouse and when it could find no way through the strange layer of the temple garment, it slid back out and into the light and felt her chest through all three layers. If this bothered or shocked Lucas, his voice gave no indication.

"'A baseball game that has all of the names and stats of real baseball players but also old baseball players, so you can be guys like Ted Williams and Mickey Mantle. When you play with old players the screen will look black-and-white and sometimes be shaky like in old footage.'"

Pin closed her eyes and was sure that her hands were moving independently of the rest of her. "What do you have on your minds, hands?" she asked them in her mind. When she opened her eyes again, they were just sitting there in her lap. "Cowards," she thought.

"'Also the stadiums should look like real stadiums and it shouldn't be so easy to hit home runs. And you should be able to make your own baseball players.'"

Then she wondered what it was that she was doing on the far side of the room. And why she was looking like that. Like she'd been sucking the milk out of weeds. It was just so strange. Strange because she could hear herself laughing and laughter did not typically from faces that looked like that. Had it been so long that her face forgot how? And the pizzas. Why was she holding pizzas? Strange, strange, strange. She had just looked at her hands and called them cowards and there weren't any pizzas there.

"The three of you," the other Pin said, "are, are, in cahoots!"

"Cahoots!" shouted Pin.

"Cahoots!" shouted Lucas and Ned.

Johnna threw the pizzas aside, the boxes opening midair, the pies hitting the wall and floor with greasy thwacks. Too angry for fluid movement, she stormed rigid-limbed from the living room to the bedroom, slamming the door behind her. When Lucas did not follow her, she went from bedroom to bathroom, slamming that door. And with a third slam, she was back in the bedroom.

"Wow," said Pin. "I can be a real bitch."

When the slamming finally stopped, the room itself seemed to wonder, Did that just happen? Exploded pizza was the only evidence that it had. But then it shrugged and went on about its business.

"'*DinoTech*,'" Lucas read on, the joint between his fingers oozing a thin line of smoke that swayed to the open window. "'You are a dinosaur from the future and you see only what the dinosaur sees as he fights a bunch of evil futuristic dinosaurs. As you go along, you pick up better and better futuristic armor and guns.'"

Elton John was singing some song she'd never heard before, and when she closed her eyes this time it was as though the whole universe was suddenly a beam of light and she was caught in its shine. Not because she was special but because she realized that she wasn't and that, compared to her, it was everything else that was so breathtaking. She was a dot of dust floating in this light. Floating because fear had always been her ballast in a small, mean world. She was in a gigantic world now where God would never find her and wasn't looking for her anyways. Fear was useless here and this was a better world.

"'You can shoot the futuristic guns but the controller will also let you bite as a weapon. Ned wants hero dinosaur to be an'—wow." Lucas interrupted himself. "That's not even close to how you spell *Anchylosaurus*. 'If dinosaur hero is an *Anchylosaurus*, then his tail will also be a weapon. All dinosaurs will look like a cross between dinosaurs and Robocop. It makes sense for main dinosaur villain to be a T-Rex. And they can talk.'"

She tried to tell herself that this was happiness, but knew that it wasn't. Even though she was laughing so hard her face hurt and couldn't stop laughing if it meant her life. Laughing at how ridiculous children's dreams can be. At grown women who slam doors when they lose their words. It wasn't happiness even though Ned's hands and mouth felt like nothing she'd ever felt before on the outside of her body. On the inside, this was happiness like sunsets cure cancer. The moment wasn't even over yet and it was already like everything else she'd ever wanted. Hard to find and not enough.

That wasn't to say she was going to stop Ned. Or herself. Because nothing else had worked either.

There was going to be a tomorrow tomorrow. No getting around that, though they tried for a while. The dark and dizzy magic wheezed steady from the living room after Johnna's blowup and when everything wasn't so funny anymore, Lucas went into the bedroom to make things right again and then didn't come back. The light was on for a long time, Lucas's high-pitched apologies and Johnna's jabbing rebuffs a constant two-toned murmur that Pin and Ned did not directly mention while on their hands and knees cleaning grease and sauce from carpet and wall. It was, they decided, the least they could do.

Pin took the wall and baseboard. Ned, the carpet. Sweat dotting his temples, the sponge rolling into pieces under his weight, he scrubbed as though there were something more he might undo than a stain. He scrubbed the way Pin sometimes scrubbed her skin.

"What a mess." She puffed her bangs from her eyes.

"Getting stoned and laughing all night used to be what Lucas and I did," said Ned. "I underestimated the degree to which the Lucas I've known forever and the Lucas Johnna married really have nothing to do with one another."

"The near future is going to be a bad time to be here if you care about such things."

"I do care," he said. "I'm sad."

"Why are you sad? Because you're leaving?"

"Because I'm going to miss my friend."

If there was a new life waiting out there for Pin to find, missing what she might leave behind was not something she'd considered. Nor did she want to. Her body was growing septic on the rotten blood of former selves. If getting better were as easy as opening a vein and sluicing out only the bad, she would have done that by now. She didn't need to be reminded that it wasn't. Or how wrong she'd been before about what she needed. Or how much easier it was to bleed the body than it was putting the blood back in.

The halo lining Johnna and Lucas's door and the back-and-forth murmuring cut out in almost the same moment. They went to bed without praying—without asking for anyone's protection or forgiveness—and Pin wondered how many nights since they were married that had happened. Zero was her guess. The carpet and wall were as clean as they were going to get. For what it was worth, the room no longer resembled a crime scene and that seemed as good a reason as any to call it a night. Ned did have an early morning, after all. Wherever he was going.

It was 2:17 in the morning. Pin sat on the bed in the guest bedroom. She was alone. It was dark. Her white blouse, thin maroon cardigan, and brown skirt lay crumpled at her feet. The temple garments sat stiff on her body. The boy-cut underwear and T-shirt were next to her on the bed, laid out as though a real girl had been sleeping there and disappeared during the night. She'd been telling herself for two hours that she would do something in just two more minutes. Just two more minutes.

2:17, she thought. *Genesis* 2:17. *But of the tree of the knowledge of good and evil, thou shalt not eat of it: for in the day that thou eatest thereof thou shalt surely die.* Yes, a lot had happened, but not so much that Pin did not still know her Bible, thank you very much. Its words, those she could never lose. Just what those words used to mean and the parts of her they used to mean something to and maybe surely dying was exactly what both needed tonight. To be put out of their misery.

Maybe not, though. Because she could sit right there on that bed until dawn, for starters. Bid Ned a pleasant goodbye in the morning. Wait for Johnna to forgive Lucas, then beg for herself. Spend the next two weeks in Provo sitting with her hands in her lap on Johnna and Lucas's orange couch. Bid them goodbye and head back to a home where she was no longer her parents' daughter.

She could return to Provo for good. Re-enroll at Brigham Young and finish her degree. See Adam around town, pretend that he was no one and pretend that she did not wonder whether his new fiancée believed she was a liar or if she thought Pin deserved what Adam had done to her. She could spend all her time with Johnna and Lucas and tell herself they were equals again and that she was not some baby bird they were kind enough to care for.

She could pray to God, have faith that He was listening, that He loved her and was with her even when it seemed He'd lost all interest in this planet. She could trust Johnna and pick her life up exactly where she had left it, pretend everything wasn't different and have faith that, eventually, it wouldn't be.

Or she could go upstairs and fuck Ned Peacock and maybe that would solve everything.

Pin removed the temple garments and slid into the boy-cut underwear. Then the T-shirt. They felt cool and clean. She missed them. She opened the door and retraced her steps from the night before. Across the floorboards. Up the stairs.

No moon, the view through the round top window was the same dark as the entire attic. She sat on the bed and was close to him before she could make out his sleeping face. Yes, she thought again, more pretty than handsome. She set her hand on his heart, feeling his heartbeat and his skin. He stirred awake and inhaled deeply.

"It's me," she said.

"I can't see you." He reached out to her, feeling her forearm with his fingertips. "What kind of face are you making right now?"

"I'm not making a face," she said, taking Ned's hand into both of hers and holding it close. "Will you do something for me?"

"Yes."

"You don't know what it is."

"Yes, yes, yes, yes, yes."

"Will you pray with me?"

For several moments, Ned did nothing but breathe. "Um," he finally said.

"Will you?"

"I don't think I know how."

"You do it like this." She slid off the bed and onto the plank floor. "Get on your knees. Put your elbows on the bed and fold your fingers together."

Springs creaked under Ned's shifting weight. He rolled out of bed and knelt down next to her. "Why like this?"

"Some thoughts are meant just for me," Pin said, crossing her ankles behind her. "Some are meant for heaven. I do this so I don't confuse them."

"Is it that easy?"

"No."

"How do you know you're not praying wrong?"

"You don't."

Minutes passed. Pin's knees went numb. Her mind was radio static. Their shoulders touched. The room was cool. Heat radiated from Ned's bare skin.

"I'm praying that when we finish," whispered Ned, "you'll let me remove all your clothes."

"So am I."

Pin bowed her head and touched her brow to her folded fingers. There was no light for her eyes to adjust to. She closed them tight and the world became no darker. Somewhere, beyond the round top window, a dog barked. Another dog answered. Nothing out there could stop her from living a life that she felt good about. So long as she could figure out what kind of life that was, she'd be okay.

That's all. Just that one small thing.

I REALLY CAN'T SAY

Each time Dick Bettencourt reads a magazine article about this city or that city being the next *It* city, he picks up and moves there. With a considerable inheritance from dead parents he was never particularly close to, he's lived in four cities in as many years—Seattle, Austin, Portland, and, as of a week ago, Oxford, Mississippi. His only friend, Tobias Kilkenny, asked him once about all of the moving.

"Magazines are very insistent they know what's best for me," he said. "God knows I don't want the responsibility."

Still living in Portland, he visited Oxford for a long weekend after reading an article in *Fortune*. He learned that good catfish was remarkably similar to bad catfish, was confounded by Ole Miss sorority girls, whose skinny legs were five inches apart at the crotch as they walked (Dick sure that whatever was between them could not possibly be vaginas as he understood them), and bought the third house a real estate agent showed him.

"So, what brings you to Oxford?" asked the chubby real estate agent. Her cell phone rang with the *Sex in the City* theme music.

"A magazine article."

"Don't you just fall in love with it immediately?"

Dick stepped off the deck of the third house's backyard and into several inches of sitting water.

"Not really," he said, pulling his foot from the grassy muck. "What's all this?"

"This house shares a backyard with an ice sculptor," she said, glaring at the house across the yard. She recovered quickly. "She tosses the old pieces back here when she's done. I've asked her not to. There's more water in ice than you'd think."

"I'll take it."

It was months before he got around to selling his Portland home. But he did, finally, and on his first night in Oxford as a resident, Dick sat on his hardwood floors, surrounded by boxes he hadn't opened since Seattle, smoked, and answered a telephone call from Tobias.

"The girls here," Dick said, "their thighs are five inches apart as they walk and go straight down. Prepubescent torsos held up by stilts."

"Does that matter to you, what the girls are like?" asked Tobias. "Are you under the impression that one of them is going to mean something to you?"

"My curiosity at this point is purely scientific."

"All of this has happened before. Has it happened enough times that you can acknowledge that?"

"No."

"Then do you want me to tell you how all of this going to end or will that ruin it for you?

"Go on."

"Sooner than later there will be a she. And she might be different, but you won't be."

"Who are you talking about?"

"You," said Tobias.

"No," said Dick. The 'she?'"

"I'm not talking about the she. I'm talking about the you."

"Noted."

After Tobias hung up, Dick pulled a scarf around his neck and sat on his back porch. He didn't know Mississippi had winters. His lawn was no longer the green soup from the previous summer. Each blade of grass was glazed with frozen dew. Black, leafless trees reached jagged from the ground like the skeletal hands of buried giants. Streetlights buzzed nearby and a round Burger King sign hung in the sky like a moon.

Twenty or so ice sculptures—some clearly upright, some clearly on their sides, some not clearly anything—littered the yard like mad tombstones. Rodin's The Thinker. The Sphinx. A translucent wedding cake. The perfectly rendered curve and snap of a roaring fire.

He lit another cigarette. The house across the way was dark and still. The back room was a recent addition. A chugging generator jutted from one of the walls and four massive windows peered into black nothing.

Dick's house was a block from the Square, a rectangle of storefronts and barfronts surrounding a white and mammoth courthouse. In front of the courthouse a stone statue of a lone Confederate soldier stood atop a looming Doric phallus. Dick stopped an old couple on the sidewalk by the statue. The man was bloated and bearded, wearing an Ole Miss sweater, scarf, and stocking cap. The woman's face was almost swallowed by a mink-lined hood. Frost tipped the mink where the mouth would be on the woman's invisible face.

"Who's that?" Dick asked, pointing to the soldier.

The man looked proudly up at the statue, then back at Dick. "Why, that's the ever faithful rebel soldier," he said, the fuzzy hood nodding in agreement.

"Oh," said Dick. "That's weird, right? Losers getting statues?"

"If you want a Union statue," said the bloated, bearded man, "might I suggest heading north?" He put one hand on his companion's shoulder, the other on the small of her back, and led her away from Dick as though he'd just exposed himself.

Dick found another statue on the western side of the Square. A glaring, fedoraed, mustachioed man of bronze sitting on a park bench. He held a smoking pipe in his hand, the stem of which almost looking like an extended middle finger. A metal sign nearby read, *Oxford, Mississippi: Birthplace of William Faulkner.*

"He doesn't look very happy," Dick said to one of the skinny-legged girls he'd probably seen that summer only now wearing a parka. She said something in response, but Dick was too busy secretly trying to figure out the dynamics of her crotch to pay attention.

Dick set up his coffeemaker that night, drank black coffee, smoked a cigarette, and sat on a box labeled *silverware* that he knew wasn't filled with silverware, waiting for Tobias to call.

"Making friends?" asked Tobias.

"I don't think so."

"Though I know that what you are doing is doomed to fail, that doesn't mean I want it to be. You know that, don't you?"

"We won the Civil War," said Dick. "Didn't we?"

"Well, not you and I personally. I believe I was the Ambassador to Portugal and you were a fur-trader in Canada. Probably because you'd read a magazine about Canada."

Through his window, the ice sculptor's built-on room glowed like a paper lantern. He watched the movement inside and didn't respond to Tobias.

"You want to go," said Tobias. "Don't you?"

"Maybe."

"Remember what I said."

"Right, right. Doomed to fail. Ambassador to Canada."

It was colder than the night before. Oxford was enveloped in a thick fog and close and distant streetlights hovered about like dandelion puffs. The frosted grass crackled under his feet as he walked toward the discarded ice sculptures. He laid his coat atop a block of ice and sat cross-legged next to The Thinker.

The addition was his neighbor's workshop. Her hair was dark and long with thick bangs above her eyes, her head topped with a pair of gray earmuffs. The generated cold made both her breath and nipples visible as she chiseled the face of a man dancing with a thin-armed girl. He watched her for hours, smoking cigarette after cigarette, occasionally allowing The Thinker a drag.

"I don't own a TV," he whispered to The Thinker.

The Thinker made no reply.

"I like you," he said, holding the cigarette to The Thinker's mouth. "You're all right."

A door on the side of the workshop opened and a translucent Winston Churchill on a mechanics roller appeared. He rolled out a little further by the force of the dark-haired girl. She looked at Dick and gave Churchill a few more shoves until he collapsed onto the frozen yard with a thud.

"'History will be kind to me,'" said Dick, "'for I intend to write it.'"

The girl took off her work gloves and stuffed them into the back pocket of her jeans. "A voyeur," she said, "is a terrible thing to end up."

"I don't recall Churchill ever saying that."

"He didn't," she said. "I'm saying it to you."

"I'm a work in progress," he conceded.

"What in the fuck are you doing in my yard?" she said coolly, leaning against the corner of the addition. She closed her eyes and took several deep breaths of the cold, wet air.

"Where my yard ends and yours begins is ambiguous, I think."

"So," she said, not opening her eyes, "I guess you're in my life now. My last neighbor hated me. She was a mean old thing. We had a terrific understanding."

"What happened to her?"

"She died and no one knew it for a month."

Dick turned and looked back at his house, liking it much more than he did before. "I like a place that can keep a secret." He turned back to the girl. "You're not southern."

"Nope."

"You've probably noticed that I'm not southern either."

"Really the only thing I've noticed about you is that you've been staring at me through my windows all night," she said, stepping towards the open door of her workshop. "Let's hope it's as easy as you not doing that anymore."

Before the door shut, before the girl left him alone and switched off the light in her workshop, cloaking herself, him, and the yard in total darkness, Dick looked to where her legs and crotch connected and they were, in fact, connected as they should be.

The sun shone bright the next day and the air was biting and crisp. Dick sat on the bench in the Square next to William Faulkner, watching people amble by. They didn't seem to be coming from or going anywhere.

"Whether that's a pipe stem or you're flicking off the entire Square," Dick said, holding his cigarette to Faulkner's mouth, "I think you're the only one who knows what he's doing here."

He recognized the bloated, bearded man and his mink-faced wife from the day before. "Speaking of which," he said, flicking his cigarette into the street. He hopped off the bench and walked towards the old couple.

"You," said the bloated, bearded man squarely.

"Yes, me," said Dick. He pointed in the general direction of his home. "What's the name of the ice sculptor?"

"Her," the old man said as squarely as he'd said 'you.'

"Yes, 'her.' Do you know 'her?'"

"She would be a friend of someone like you."

"She's not my friend. I'm asking you what her name is."

"What exactly is your business in Oxford?"

"Real estate," he said. "Self-discovery, maybe."

"Turvy," said the old man, combining both great contempt and great dignity into a single thing. "Her name is Turvy."

They walked on, the old man and his gaudy Eskimo. They walked on and Dick figured if he knew where it was they were going, where any of these people were going in the middle of the afternoon, he'd have a better idea if he belonged here or not. Other than away from him, the man and woman didn't seem to be going anywhere.

He sat again that night next to The Thinker, watching Turvy through the wide windows of her workshop as she honed and made fine the lines and curves of the dancing partners. Churchill still lay on his side by the door, whole and noble, as though he might get up himself in but a moment.

Turvy came out at about one. She looked at him and shook her head.

"Who was it that gave you that ridiculous name?" he asked her. "Parents? Yourself? Was it to make you seem more interesting?"

"I just need some air," she said. She folded her fingers behind her head and cracked her back.

"What I'm getting at is that I would think you're interesting even if your name was Amanda or one of those other names people have."

"There isn't a single thing about myself that I value that you know the first thing about."

"You're welcome," he said.

"I miss the mean old dead woman," said Turvy. "The entire block stewing in her rot vapor. I never thought I'd miss that, but after these little chats of ours."

"My name's Dick," he said, and pointed to the upturned Churchill. "Was he insolent?"

"I need the room."

Dick nodded towards her windows. "For Fred and Ginger?"

"Those aren't their names."

"You're very good."

"You're bizarre. You make me uncomfortable. If you watch me tomorrow, I'll call the police." She disappeared into her workshop.

"I know, man," he said to The Thinker. "Not very neighborly."

The starless sky the next night pissed slushy rain. Dick wore a yellow rain slicker and put one of his blazers around The Thinker's shoulders. He sat on an Ole Miss stadium-cushion he bought on the Square. Turvy wasn't wearing her gray earmuffs. She wore instead a telephone headset, speaking to someone, looking perturbed as she worked on the dancers with a hammer and chisel.

"I wonder who she's talking to," he said. "It doesn't seem natural, idle chit-chat while in the act of artistic creation. It's like calling your mother amidst a carnal act."

Turvy started talking loud. The conversation deteriorated quickly and she threw off the headset. She dropped her chisel and started pounding on the dancing couple, shattering the girl's arm, pummeling the neck and face of the man until it refused to lose any more significant chunks. Breathing hard, Turvy collapsed onto the floor, at the feet of Fred and Ginger and out of sight.

Dick picked up some ice chips from the ground and tossed them at the window. There was no movement from inside. He did it again. Turvy opened the side door and walked out, her arms hanging heavy.

"You all right?" he said.

She looked at The Thinker wearing Dick's blazer.

"He was cold," Dick said. "Feel him. He's like ice."

"Now's not a good time for whatever it is that you are."

"Were you calling the police on me and you're angry because they're not coming because no one in this town likes you?"

"Seriously," she said, pinching the bridge of her nose with a gloved hand.

"Seriously, yourself. I had a deep emotional investment in the conception of Fred and Ginger, and I want to know what was so much more important."

"I shouldn't have done that," she conceded. Dick could see her trying to undo what just happened, reassembling the man and woman with her mind.

"You should have known better," said Dick. "I was just saying, it didn't seem right to do that kind of work while on the phone. Like it was just another chore. Scouring the tub or throwing out old cereal or whatever else it is that people do."

"My husband's not coming here for Christmas."

"Really?" said Dick. "Is Christmas coming up?"

"He lives in Atlanta. It's a six hour drive."

"You're not talking to me right now, are you?"

"What kind of man—" Turvy started, then said nothing.

"It's not Christmas today, is it?"

"Are you even listening to me?"

Dick stood, Turvy looking a little surprised that he could, the stadium-cushion sucking in air as he rose. "Are you listening to you?" he said, walking into and past her personal space. He stood in the doorway and looked at the pulverized dancers.

"That's you and him," he said. "Right?"

"We've been known to dance."

"I bet he's in a band and fucks lots of girls who think he's not like all of the other guys who cheat on their wives."

"He can't commit to our break-up. He wants us to end. He wants me to do it. My last gift to him is forcing him to be man enough to do it himself."

Dick stepped into the workshop and thought it funny how it got colder as he did. He wiped flakes and specks of ice from the woman's fine-lined face.

"Whatever happened to men and women?" he said. "Didn't it used to mean something?"

From outside, Turvy made no reply.

"Probably not," he said to no one.

Turvy entered the doorway. He continued cleaning ice from the girl's face.

"You know what I like about you?" he said. "You like blocks of ice more than people. I get that."

"You look like a big banana."

Dick slid his wet hands across his wet slicker and conceded that, yes, he probably did. "It's not Christmas today," he said again. "Is it? I know it's in December. Is it December?"

"It'll be Christmas next week."

He walked towards Turvy. "That's enough time for him to come around."

"He won't."

"No," he said. "He won't."

Dick took off the glove on Turvy's left hand. The skin on each finger nearest the nails and knuckles were cracked and bleeding. Her wedding ring was white-gold with a marquis-cut diamond.

"What in the fuck is that?"

"What?"

"That's not the sort of ring a girl wants," he said. "I've seen lots of pictures of rings girls want and that is not one of them."

"It's not very handsome."

"Will you be working in here on Christmas?"

"Yes," she said, taking off the other glove.

"Wanna hang out?"

"Will you be out there anyway?"

"Yes."

"There's something wrong with you, isn't there?" Turvy asked. "Deeply and irrevocably wrong."

"You're married to a man who would rather spend Christmas in Atlanta than with you. Turvy, I've been to Atlanta."

She chewed on the inside of her cheek and looked at nothing. She was done that day dealing with sentences.

"Tired," she finally said.

He gave her a clipped bow in a gesture of goodnight. He left the blazer around the The Thinker's shoulders. Somewhere in his house there was a box full of blazers labeled, if Dick remembered correctly, *Democracy*.

From inside his dark kitchen, through cracked blinds, he watched Turvy's house close up shop. The backyard sculptures—The Thinker, the Sphinx, Churchill, the wedding cake, all of them—caught the workshop's bright light and glowed like bar bottles. The workshop lights went out and the shapes were lost to the night. A bedroom light went on and again the pieces glowed, but faintly. When the bedroom light went out, the darkness stuck.

Dick's eyes adjusted until he was staring at his own reflection in the window. He had never before seen himself excited by whatever was going to happen next.

Dick arranged the boxes containing all of his worldly possessions, most of which he'd long forgotten existed, into an elaborate fort in his sunken living room. He wrote *Xanadu* on one of the outer walls with a Sharpie and wondered for hours which room of the house the former owner had died in. Then if she owned any dogs or cats that snacked on her while she rotted and, if so, who, other than himself, would want such a pet. In the animal world, was such a thing redeemable?

That's not a thing that's obvious, he thought, whether or not your pet would eat you if you died. But, then again, people all the time seem to be able to look at a thing and not just see the thing, but what's inside the thing. Turvy can do it. Figuratively and literally. She can look at a block of ice the size of a refrigerator, see what's inside, and then let it out.

Of course, when she's done she tosses them out into her yard. Was that part of the metaphor?

Giving all of this intense thought, Dick hadn't left Xanadu for thirty-six hours, except to use the bathroom, when Tobias called.

"Did you build a fort yet?" he asked.

"I did," said Dick. "What kind of boyfriend do you think I'd make?"

"The kind who is incapable of either giving or experiencing love."

"Fair enough. What state are you in?" asked Dick. "I mean, really, in regards to the country. What are you doing and where are you doing it?"

It was rare for Dick to ask Tobias a direct question about his life. He seemed confused. "I'm in upstate New York," he finally said. "I'm dating a girl who's been committed to an insane asylum."

"Do they still call them that?" asked Dick. "'Insane asylums?'"

"I don't know. That's what I call them."

"It sounds like you're dating a Batman villain. Is she a Batman villain?"

"Is self-mutilation a superpower?"

"If it is, it's not a great one. Then again, the Riddler's superpower was telling Batman about the crimes he was going to commit."

"I visit her every day. She likes Spencer Tracy. I bring her Spencer Tracy-related gifts. I tell her about the times that were good and how they're going to be good again someday. It's tough."

"I imagine there are fewer Spencer Tracy-related items on the market than you'd think."

"You don't understand. You'll never understand. But that's not the problem. The problem is that you always forget that you'll never understand."

"There's this girl," said Dick.

"I know there is. And her life is a mess in a way that utterly fascinates you. Like you just graduated college and she's a trip to Kenya."

"Have you heard good things about Kenya?"

"Most people, their lives are just a stinking mess. And they take up with other people whose lives are stinking messes so they won't have to go through it alone. And battling these messes together, that becomes their lives."

"Why do they want to do that?"

"My girlfriend cuts herself and calls me to tell me what the blood looks like. And I always answer the phone. Trust me when I say this isn't what any of us wants."

"And that's your life?"

"That's my life."

"What's my life?"

"All clean lines and fresh starts. And this girl, your girl, she's just a vacation. You'll never need her. And if you let it get to the point where she needs you, you'll be long gone." Through the receiver, Dick heard Tobias scratch his head then collapse into a chair. "So, really, what is it that you think you can give her that no one else in the world can?"

"You mean, like, for Christmas?"

"No, Dick. That isn't what I mean."

*

Dick bought a kittens-wrapped-in-fresh-laundry calendar the next day and asked the checkout girl what day it was. He wrote Friday on his hand with the same Sharpie he used to write Xanadu, went home, and pinned the calendar to the wall of his fort. Christmas, so said the calendar, was on Monday. He crossed off Friday.

For the first half of Saturday, he hooked up a radio inside Xanadu and sat listening to Christmas music. It wasn't hard for him to pull out the recurring themes. Just barely getting through the rest of the year because there's this one day to look forward to. When that day comes, and if you can't be with the people you want to be with, or where, or when, memories of this glowing past keep you moving forward.

And there was this one about a kid who gives a newborn a drum solo for Christmas that seems to go over pretty well, though the song itself did not feature a noteworthy drum solo.

If Dick was going to prove Tobias wrong about him, if he truly was capable of being enveloped into the lives of others, this was the time. People were primed for that sort of thing. He understood what all those people shambling about the Square were doing. They were looking for that perfect thing—a physical object—to give the people in their lives that would say what their words couldn't the rest of the year.

He spent the second half of Saturday shopping on the Square. He bought an XXL Ole Miss sweater, a snorkel, the Abraham Lincoln biography that insinuated he was a homosexual, and pipe tobacco. He went home, crossed off Saturday, and wrapped each gift in maps he found in his glove compartment.

On Sunday, he set the Lincoln biography at the base of the Confederate soldier statue. He placed the pipe tobacco on Faulkner's lap, sat next to him, and waited. When the bloated, bearded man and his parkaed wife passed by, he jumped up and gave them the sweater and snorkel.

"Don't open these until Christmas," he said. They took the parcels slowly and moved on. "It's tomorrow," Dick shouted after them.

He went home and crossed off Sunday. He went through one of his bags and pulled out a never-worn button-down, a tie, and a v-neck sweater the girl who sold it to him in Portland referred to as "very smart." He disassembled one of Xanadu's walls and rooted through boxes until he found his iron in a box labeled *Revolutionary Era Figurines* and unfolded his ironing board.

"Where in the fuck did I get an ironing board?"

Dick ironed his shirt, his tie, the sweater, for good measure, and showered thoroughly though he already had that morning. He dressed, slipped on a pair of mittens and, at midnight, walked out his backdoor, onto his porch, crunched through the pale grass, and sat next to The Thinker.

"Merry Christmas," he said to The Thinker. "It's Christmas right now."

The Thinker melted slightly that day then refroze. He was now molecularly entwined with the blazer and would be until spring forever rendered them asunder them.

Turvy came out of her workshop a while later. She wore a child's toboggan, a brown sweater, her work gloves, and well-worn jeans. She put her hands on her hips. He lit a cigarette. He heard wind chimes.

"Not working tonight?" Dick finally said through an exhale of smoke.

"I don't feel like working," she said. "I work every night."

"I'm wearing a very smart sweater."

"You look like Paul Newman with red hair."

"Really?" Dick pushed his hand through his hair a few times. "Yeah, I guess it is red."

"How do you smoke with mittens on?" she asked.

"I smoke in the shower."

They looked at each other for a while, as though both were waiting for a third party to direct them.

"We're being ridiculous," Turvy said, ushering Dick to his feet. "Come inside."

Dick hadn't really taken in the interior of the workshop the week before. Three five-foot pillars of ice lined the far wall. Ice shavings covered the cement floor like snow.

"Do you wanna know something about me?" Turvy said, shutting the door behind her. The door leading into the original frame of the house was also shut. "I wasn't planning on being married before thirty and now I'll be divorced before it."

"You could have gone to Atlanta," said Dick.

"No. I couldn't have."

"You married a musician who buys white-gold, marquis-cut diamond engagement rings," Dick said, turning towards her. "You sorta had it coming."

"He's not a musician," she said.

"Is he a DJ at a club? A soldier? A coke dealer? He's one of those things that tricks girls like you into marrying."

"And who's a girl like me?"

"A girl who'd probably achieve great things if not held down by a mediocre man who continues to look around even after conquering a girl like you because, after all, if he was man enough to conquer a girl like you, why shouldn't he think he could conquer two or three?"

"You seem very sure and pointed."

"I know I do," said Dick. "I also know that none of it matters very much."

"Everything matters. Every choice I've ever made drags behind me like an anchor." She walked about the room, sliding her fingers along the walls. "For a while, my workshop was a safe place. When I was in here, there wasn't anything else."

"I'm not sure there is," said Dick. "I just sorta take peoples' word for it."

"You have to do very little to make tonight nice," she said. "All you have to do is not be the worst man on earth."

He walked the two steps separating them and took her left hand into his. "You know what your problem is? Well, first of all, this." He removed the work glove and slid the white-gold, marquis-cut ring from her finger, flipped it into the corner, and slid her glove back on. "That's better. Second—"

"I really can't imagine what you're about to say."

"—here you are trying to outrun a big, stupid world. A marriage.

Mississippi. This house in Mississippi. This room in this house. All those things worked for a while. Maybe it's time to dig in a little deeper."

Dick went into the house and returned with an armful of blankets. He draped one of the blanket ends over the dancers and the other end over an ice block. Underneath the jerry-rigged tent, he spread out the rest of the blankets over the bed of ice shavings.

"Come on then," he said, poking his head out from the billows.

They huddled up close in the cold dark. This isn't so bad, he thought. She thought so too, he decided, feeling her body untense next to his.

"It's quiet," she said.

"Yeah, the world's really not that hard to get away from."

"Are you kidding? It's impossible."

"Why not? There's more than enough blankets."

"If we tried to do this tomorrow, all we'd be doing is comparing then to right now and it won't be the same."

"I won't be doing that."

"You said I like blocks of ice more than people. That's not true. I try to make them more than what they are, but it's never enough. Each time the living world pulls me back, it's not enough all over again."

"That sounds exhausting."

"It is. This is nice though." She burrowed into him, resting her head on his shoulder. "Maybe I'll carve this someday."

That was the last thing she said that night. There was a crack of light all around them where blanket just barely touched floor. When his eyes adjusted, Dick saw they were not alone. Fred and Ginger loomed over them in the almost-dark. Battered. Glistening.

He awoke in the workshop next to a sleeping Turvy. Her lips were blue and he imagined his were as well. He walked with her in his arms through her house, into and out of rooms until he found her bedroom. He set her down on her bed, removed her gloves, toboggan, and cocooned her in covers.

Photographs festooned the room. Lining the walls. Plaquing the vanity mirror. Shelves jagged with frames like crooked teeth. They were all of Turvy and some man who could have been any man. The sedimentary layers of two lives entwined. Two teenagers posing at prom. Two bronzy, glossy-skinned college kids in front of the Sphinx. Her in a white dress, him in a tuxedo. All around him, as clear as anything, were the distances he'd never go to. The time he'd never give. The sacrifices he'd never make. And how, at the end of it, Turvy was still alone. An alone he wanted no part of, in a prison of everything that's come before.

He left the room. Before exiting the house through the workshop door, he knelt down, picked up Turvy's wedding ring, and slipped it into his pocket.

The next day, Dick walked to a hardware store and bought a sledgehammer, then a jeweler where he bought a platinum ring with a round-cut diamond. He went home and checked the mail slot in his front door and found a pile of pennysavers and unread magazines. He bundled the magazines under his arm and sat in Xanadu until early evening.

Sitting Indian-style, he flipped through the magazines. There were pictures of men wearing clothes he'd never wear, analyses of sports cars, articles with headlines like *The Top Ten Things You Should Do in Vegas and Never Tell Your Wife About*, and layouts of women Dick guessed were famous in various stages of pout and undress. It took three hours for Dick to find what he was looking for. *Details* proclaiming Minneapolis *The Next Big It City.*

Tobias called.

"How are things wherever the hell you are?" Tobias asked.

"Bad day in *It* city. How's your Batman villain?"

"Today was a good day."

"What makes days like yours good?"

"When they're better than all the other days."

"And that's enough?"

"I'm thankful for days like today."

Dick held the ring he'd stolen from Turvy. It really was very ugly. It felt ugly. Atlanta's ugly too. He's never read anything good about Atlanta.

"I'm thankful for magazines," said Dick.

"Where to next?"

"What do you know about Minneapolis?"

"Very little," Tobias said. "I know, generally speaking, that Minnesota is where ugly people come from."

Just after sunset, Dick picked up the sledgehammer and walked out onto his and Turvy's backyard. He knocked The Thinker's head clean off his shoulders and set the platinum, round-cut diamond ring on the neck stump. He left the sledgehammer leaning against The Thinker and carried the head to his house.

"Minneapolis," he said to The Thinker's head, leaning against the open freezer. "*The Next Big It City*. That sounds hard to believe, but this is *Details* we're talking about."

Half awake, half asleep that night in Xanadu, Dick thought he heard the sledgehammer knocking Fred and Ginger into oblivion. But he knew better. The ring. The framed photographs. Atlanta. Put all the terrible pieces together and you get the man Turvy loves. And she does love this man. And will for much longer than is good for anyone involved.

No, Fred and Ginger weren't going anywhere. But he was.

Tomorrow he'll buy a dog-tag chain and wear Turvy's awful ring around his neck, a reminder that the only life for him is the life ahead. Then he'll call a real estate agent in Minneapolis. And beyond that, well, there was nothing beyond that.

WHERE ARE YOU
IN RELATION TO ME?

HE DIDN'T REMEMBER HIS PARENTS BEING MARRIED. HIS FATHER WANTED to be his friend. His mother wanted quiet while she napped on the couch or watched *M*A*S*H*. His earliest memories were of his grandmother. They ate goose-liver sandwiches and built puzzles. She told him what love was and that there was some little girl out in the world that he'd love someday and for the rest of his life. He tried but could not picture her face, this girl he'd never seen, a gauzy snapshot in his mind.

The first girl he kissed was the first girl in high school to get a tattoo. Her name was Carly and it was a rose on her ankle. Everything she owned—her clothes, her car, the letters she wrote him—smelled of the Mexican restaurant she worked at on the weekends. Carly's ex-boyfriend's name was Dean. Her letters said she didn't love Dean anymore and they weren't together and they'd never be together again. He was the only one who believed her. The letters stopped.

*

Paula was the first girl to have a crush on him in college. She sat next to him in Calculus. Like the girls he'd known in high school, she seemed to work hard at being thin and blonde. Unlike them, she considered spatial reasoning a virtue and followed baseball. She asked him to play catch with her. He couldn't. Paula must have worked in a Mexican restaurant. She smelled like Carly and everything Carly owned. He would find it funny, eventually and too late, how a girl he'd never talk to again could ruin him for a girl he'd not met yet. Not ha-ha funny. But, still, funny.

His sophomore year in college, he harbored illusions of waiting until marriage. Not that he was religious. He just thought that would make it mean something. But Eva never wore clothes. In her apartment. In his apartment. It was a three-party romance. Him. Eva. And Eva's body. He sat on a couch, reading. Naked, she knelt before him and kissed his feet. He lowered the book. In between her blonde bangs and his toes in her mouth, Eva's big eyes looked up into his. "Lay down," he said.

Meredith was a Christian who had been on the cover of *Blackbook Magazine*. They kissed and kissed, but he wasn't allowed to lie on top of her. Nor was he allowed to touch her on her "red light areas." They were together one evening, side by side on her bed, kissing closed-mouthed. She broke away, leaned up, and pointed at the half-erection in his pants.

"What is it with you and those things?" she said. "Why is your body so bent on disrespecting me?" You must have one of those faces, he didn't say. Everyone told him how lucky he was to be dating a model.

He took a semester off to work an internship in the South. The night he met Imogen, she told him of the time she visited cousins in London and how they did too many drugs in their flat and she passed out. Thinking she was dead, her cousins put her in a dumpster.

"Christmases must be awkward," he said.

After they made love, she lay naked on his aerobed, the room and her body lit by a warm desk lamp. She pointed to a pair of his underwear and said, "Put those on me." Floating her legs above the sheets, then her pelvis, he slid them onto her.

"You make me feel like a ring finger," she said.

She slept right there that night, and every night for a week. On the eighth night, she stopped returning his calls.

He and Sallie-Cathy interned together. She was pretty, funny, and wore her hair in two long braids. Her boss never assigned her work and, to pass the time, she'd sometimes walk the halls like Robocop. Sometimes like a snooty waiter. This was how she lived.

When they crossed a bridge while driving somewhere, she'd say, "Hold your breath until we get to the other side." Imogen fresh on his mind, he found Sallie-Cathy's goodness boring. He was distracted when they were together. He'd forget he was holding his breath halfway across and start breathing again. Years later, he'd wonder how that was possible.

When Imogen did finally call, she said she loved him and had made a terrible mistake and that she had never broken things off with a boyfriend but that he was now history.

That night, she slept in his bed wearing his underwear.

The next night she talked about an art school in London she'd be attending in the fall.

The next night, she talked incessantly of the ex-boyfriend. He dealt coke. He was twenty-nine. He'd been in a band that had a hit. Juliana Hatfield had written a song about him. She left his apartment before it got too late.

She stopped returning his calls. His internship ended and he went back home.

*

Junior year, he lay stomach down on Ginny's bed, drinking Pabst tall boys as they watched a reality show about regular people trying to become famous. Empties clinking and clanking, Ginny rolled over atop of him, her front pressed to his back. She leaned in so close to his ear, he could smell her lipstick.

"If I had a penis," she said, "I could fuck you in the ass." In that moment, he wished she had a penis.

Brea liked her job more than she liked him. She worked at Nordstrom. She sold him a pair of shoes. When she came to his apartment at night, she'd want to have sex quick because she had to open in the morning. She smelled like many perfumes and Italian leather. She smelled like his mother's purse. She loved him like his mother, too. On the fly. Thoughts of his mother. Thoughts of her. He couldn't separate the two. He conceded that he probably could have if he tried. Breaking it off was easier.

Imogen emailed him. "Visit me." When he stepped off the jetway at Heathrow and saw Imogen's faux-hawk, he knew she was still dating musicians. When he saw how skinny she was, he knew she was still addicted to something. When she threw her arms around his neck and squeezed tightly, he knew this was going to end poorly.

His grandmother passed away. She was buried next to his grandfather and his great-grandmother and great-grandfather. He walked through Greenlawn cemetery and almost all of the headstones belonged to the "Missed," the "Beloved," the "Reunited at Last." The ones that didn't, the monuments to nothing, made him very sad. He tried again to conjure the image of the girl his grandmother told him about. She was older. She was aging with him. That much he could tell. The rest was still blurry.

*

Rose was the first girl he called his girlfriend. In bed, late at night, underneath the sheets, sometimes they pretended to be brother and sister.

"We shouldn't do this anymore."

"Don't tell Mom."

Rose doesn't really have a brother, he told himself. And he had no sisters. So that made it OK. Right? Her psychologist suggested they separate.

He graduated and made a list titled *One-Hundred Things I Shall Do Before I Die*. *Swim in a swimming hole* was on his list. He worked with Elizabeth. She was raised in a small town, had been in 4-H, and loved the sound of diesel engines. She took him to a watering hole near her family's home. They took off their clothes. The water was icy and tasted like copper. Her body was round and soft. Like a pink, fluffy cloud. He wanted to jump into her, to bundle her up tight and use her for a pillow. Many thoughts involving touching her. But he wouldn't. Her ankles were too thick.

Cherry was the second girl he called his girlfriend. They divided their time between two tiny apartments and bottles of wine. She had six-shooters tattooed to her hips and punched him in the face while they made love. When he agreed to watch her go down on another man, he knew he'd never be able to look at her again. He was right.

Imogen called and said she loved him and had made a terrible mistake and that she had been kicked out of the London art school and was back in the South. She picked him up at the airport wearing a thrift store t-shirt so threadbare only her nipples were covered. Taking the highway to Imogen's new apartment, they crossed a wide river. "I bet I can hold my breath until we get to the other side," he said. Lungs full, blood thumping in his brain, he thought of Sallie-Cathy for the first time in years. He wondered where she was, how she was, if he could ever find her if he tried, almost blacking out before realizing Imogen had slowed the car to fifteen miles per hour.

In Turkish, Eren is a boy's name. It was the only boyish thing about her, long and willowy and betrothed to a man on the other side of the world serving his required military time just outside of Istanbul. They shopped in an expensive boutique, her spending the fiancé's money. In the window, a mannequin with Eren's long and lean body wore black and white striped, thigh-high leggings and pink underwear.

While Eren picked things off the rack and rolled her eyes, he watched the mannequin. While Eren disheveled folded piles, he imagined peeling down the leggings and burying his face into a betrothed pelvis, knowing he never would and that she probably wouldn't even let him. Not because she wasn't promiscuous. Because he wasn't Muslim.

He married. She came from a wealthy family. She enjoyed being poor for a while. Then she didn't. Her father found him a different job and oversaw the transition from renting to owning.

Through the course of one thing becoming another, he heard that Carly never stopped working at the Mexican restaurant, had gone on anti-depressants and gained over a hundred pounds.

He never heard from Paula but assumed she did not still work at a Mexican restaurant, if she ever did.

Meredith moved to Seattle and was a founding member of a "church" from which he sometimes received "literature."

Eva became a favorite of photographer Richard Kern and was prominently featured in the coffee table book *Whore Chic* published by Tacshen.

Ginny was a recovering alcoholic living in California, the oldest waitress in a German restaurant where the milkmaid uniforms pressed her breasts up to her chin.

He still has the shoes Brea sold him, though he never wears them.

He never heard from Rose but has a recurrent dream of her and her psychologist laughing at him.

Elizabeth married a manatee expert and they spend their time touring zoos and aquariums.

Cherry died of leukemia and, at her funeral, the only face he recognized was the man they'd invited into their bedroom. "This is harder on me than you, I guess," said the other man. "I mean, you broke up with her."

Eren moved to Istanbul, married her fiancé, divorced him two years later, moved back to the states, married another Turkish man, divorced again, and married a Jewish sports agent.

His phone rang one day. It was an area code from the South. "Sallie-Cathy?" he said. No. It was a friend of Imogen's he barely remembered. Imogen had been in rehab and, just before getting out, she drove off with an ex-boyfriend. A week later she was found in the dumpster of a Motel 6, blue and wearing only track-marks and a pair of boys underwear. The friend thought he should know.

That night, ten years before he and his wife would divorce, he walked expressionless through their house, through the living room where she lay on a couch watching TV. He stood in the den for several minutes, then walked back through the living room and into the kitchen. He stood in the dark room staring into the open refrigerator, an angle of light dissecting the tan linoleum. He laughed, polite and low. The kind of laugh that's easy to spell. Heh, heh, heh.

"What's funny?" his wife asked from the next room.

"Nothing," he said, the gauzy image of the girl in his mind coming into sharp focus. She wore her hair in two long braids. "Nothing is funny."

THE OLD MAN,
THE MAN,
AND THE YOUNG MAN

THE OLD MAN, THE MAN, AND THE YOUNG MAN. THEY WERE, ALL THREE of them, thinking about death. Maybe it was the dead man on the pool table. Maybe it was the two hundred mourners crowding the bar, singing, telling stories, saying, "No one drinks Bud tonight. He fucking hated Bud." Most of them were surprised it wasn't the old man's turn on the green felt. No one more so than the old man himself. He wrapped his arm around the neck of the young man and said into his ear, "I've been dodging death for seven years. I maybe have two left. We lost a good one today."

The myth of the old man was larger than the town. The novels that almost won him the Pulitzer. The trouble he'd caused as a drunk. Like the time he was arrested for throwing knives into the door of the museum. "But they were old knives," he told the newspaper. Or the time he shot holes into the floor of his convertible to drain the water after a hard rain. That was a long time ago. Before the cancer. Before the heart disease.

"Before I quit drinking," he said, stirring a Screwdriver with his finger.

He held court, telling stories about the dead man that made death just
another kind of life. To his right sat the man—borderline famous, borderline
alcoholic—who had dedicated his last book to the old man. To his left, the
young man, adrift somewhere in his first novel and who had moved to the
town hoping to experience nights like this.

The bartenders were already clearing the tables when paramedics came
and took the dead man back to the funeral home to a chorus of "Suwannee
River." He had been the chief of police, the dead man, and the old man was
mid story—the one about the dead man confiscating his harpoon gun—when
the bartenders politely asked him and everyone to wrap things up.

"Fucking philistines," said the man, paying his and the old man's tabs.

"Pimps," said the old man. "Bourgeoisie fucks."

They stepped outside and walked arm-in-arm underneath a sickled
copper moon, across the square, singing songs the words to which the young
man did not know. The man had been reading the old man's books for
twenty years, known him for ten, watched the chemo turn his muscles into
meringue, and could feel his hollow bones against his ribs and draped across
his shoulder. The old man took his arm off the young man, made a gun with
his fingers, pointed it at a streetlight and said, "Bang."

At the cars, the man asked the old man, who couldn't hold it like he
used to, if he needed a ride home. "What I need is fewer bored cops," he said.
"Another DUI. The biographers would just love that."

The young man drove the old man's Chrysler, the old man slumped
shotgun—saying how fucking sad and early it was, how the dead man was
owed a bender for the ages—the man following behind. The young man had
been to his home once before, to move a TV, refusing payment until it became
awkward. He relented, took the twenty-dollar bill, went home and folded it
into the pages of his journal like a sweetheart's flower.

"I'm going to ask the two of you in for some beers," said the old man in
his driveway, hoisting himself out of the car. "It gets lonesome here."

Two babies and a wife waiting for him at home and the man still couldn't tell the old man no. If he knew his apartment was on fire, the young man would not have declined.

The house built like a train, each room conjoined longways to the next, they walked to the old man's study. Six mongrel dogs wiggling at their feet, the rooms became increasingly cluttered, lived in, the first few still holding onto the woman's touch of the old man's third and deceased wife.

They filed into the study by decreasing drunkness, the old man first, the young man last. The old man sat at his desk, laced a breathing tube behind his ears, around his face, and lit a Camel Wide, all at the same time. The man sat on a couch that looked like a rat's nest made of Navajo blankets. The young man moved a trombone to the floor and sat in a rocking chair. They cracked three Miller High-Lifes.

"It's not our own deaths we fear," the old man said. "It's the deaths of those we love."

"He was more a part of this town than the dirt," the man said, raising his bottle. In his heart he toasted the dead man's laugh, how the bar was empty without it. The wicked light in the old man's eyes back when he thought himself invincible. His own wife's frown back when she expected him to come home when he said he would.

On any given day, the young man envied the two men's genius. That night, he envied too their sadness. He wished he had known the dead man, had shaken his hand at least once. That his misery was real, which it would be, in time.

"I've buried three wives," said the old man.

"To be fair," said the man, "you weren't married to two of them at the time."

"That doesn't make them any less buried." He bowed for nearly a minute, chin to chest. The man and the young man shrugged at one another. "If I still felt it like I used to," he finally said, lifting his head, grinning like a mad bomber, "I'd be fucking your wife."

"She'd love it."

"An antique like me?" He pointed to the young man with his cigarette. "You. You're virile. Why aren't you fucking his wife?"

"I dunno," he said, then looked to man. "What do you think?"

"Someone ought to be fucking her."

When the laughter settled and the room's only sound was the chug of the oxygen concentrator, the man asked about the old man's son. The young man was surprised there was a son.

"In Birmingham. Married to a fucking sociopath. Not calling on Father's Day." Moving slow, as if underwater, the old man smoked the cigarette down to the nub and lit a second off the cherry. "Three things I never wanted for him."

"How's the book?" asked the young man.

The old man looked like he was doing math in his head, then said, "Want to hear some of it?" Before they could say yes, they absolutely would, the old man was up, walking bowlegged and wooden to the next room, the clear plastic tube trailing behind.

It had been five years, a dead wife, a cancer diagnosis, and three missed deadlines since the last book. For two of the five, the old man swore it was almost finished. Returning to the study, the manuscript tucked under one bony arm, he swore this again.

In that room, lit by one brass desk lamp, the walls festooned with awards, the shelves packed with books and handguns, the old man read. It was the story of a man who found Jesus Christ and love, lost them both, but thought they might be coming round again. Eyes closed, the man and the young man listened hard. To the power and grace of a soul that, though trapped in a withering husk, could still lift houses off the ground.

"I'm only worthy when I write," said the old man when he finished. "I know this."

The old man, crumpled in his chair, cadaverous, loll-eyed, told the man and the young man that they were, "Captains. My co-pilots." The man and the young man left. It was time. Time for the man to be with his sleeping family. Time for the young man to go home and write it all down.

He did. And he wrote it wrong. Leaving out how the man went home, decided not to wake his sleeping wife to tell her that he loved her, and fell asleep on the floor of his babies' dinosaur-wallpapered room. Leaving out which of those handguns the old man would one day clean and oil before firing it into his own brain. Or which person who didn't love him anymore he was thinking about when he did. Or how, that night, the old man sat in his chair, thought of the dead man, and wept.

But he couldn't have known these things. Even if he could, he wouldn't have understood. That would come much later. The old man and the man long dead. An old man himself.

It was wrong because what he wrote was not a sad story.

PETER IN CHAINS

EUGENE MERIDIAN'S ONLY WIFE WAS BORN IN 1933. HER PARENTS, New Dealers to their bones, named her Nira and were proud to have done so long after the Supreme Court ruled the National Industrial Recovery Act unconstitutional. Something in them, Nira told her husband on more than one occasion, died with President Roosevelt. Eugene, lean and twenty when his CO broke the news of the grand old man's passing, had only so much time to think about it while he and the men of Dog Company drove eastward through Germany. Hitler died in a dank, artillery-blasted bunker, two bombs fell in Japan, Eugene went home, and six years later, he and Nira met at college and were married. He founded Meridian-Flint and retired after forty-five years at a drafting table. He bought her an Edward Hopper original for their fifty-first anniversary. Nira promised him she would live to see their fifty-second.

She didn't.

Alone in the house he designed and built for her, filled with her books and his framed blueprints, he went days without hearing his own voice. No children. Flint long dead. Most of the old friends dead, too, or dying, or unrecognizable. Eugene spent the dawns of several weeks as a mall walker. The other old men, in their ballcaps and windbreakers, talked of grandchildren and heart disease, of which Eugene had neither. And when the talk turned to old wars, which the talk always did, eventually, Eugene had trouble believing a word they said. The old men told the tall tales common to jeep jockeys and swab hands. The kind of stories that, if they were true, were kept close and in the dark. Eugene knew, and probably so did they, that he was not one of them and began stopping short of the mall, pulling instead into the parking lot of a Barnes and Noble.

The first customer through the door every morning, Eugene chose an arm full of books—Twain, Poe, history books about wars he hadn't fought— and sat alone in the café with a large coffee and a scone. Two, three hours a day, every day. Other than Nina Simone or Bob Dylan drifting overhead, the barista sitting on a stool behind the bar, and one other regular, the café was a ghost town.

The other regular was in his late twenties. He wore dark, pegged jeans and his hair up in a pompadour. He was broad-boned, a cross between a fifties tough and a circus strongman. He walked through the door several minutes after Eugene, ordered coffee, and leafed through glossy art books he pulled from the shelves—Kandinsky, Pollock, Goldsworthy—two tables down. One morning, as Eugene sat rereading some Hemingway, fat snow burying the empty parking lot beyond the windows, the other regular spoke.

"He's good," he said, nodding towards Eugene's *A Moveable Feast*.

"He is." Eugene motioned towards the young man's *The Great Works of Frank Lloyd Wright*. "So is he."

"Yup," he said, licking his thumb and turning a page.

After his two or three hours at Barnes and Noble, Eugene would drive to the local natatorium to swim laps and practice his water tai chi, which he didn't have to do. He owned a pool. Indoor. Heated. Though, really, the pool was more Nira's than his. He paid a man to keep it chlorinated and clean, but didn't use it, just as he didn't talk about Edward Hopper or walk the hallway the painting hung in. He didn't read Fitzgerald, Nira's favorite author. He avoided the smell of Chanel No. 5 when he could and knew he would never again eat cherries jubilee.

*

Eugene and the other regular shared the café five more days in silence, two, three tables apart. Six days since they spoke, the other regular walked into the Barnes and Noble, shook snow from his wool pea coat, ordered coffee, sat with Eugene like that's how it always was between them and opened a book of noir movie posters.

"Morning," said the other regular.

"Morning," said Eugene. They shook hands.

"Nathan Dauer," he said, looking down at his book.

"Eugene Meridian," said Eugene, scanning the page of his Abraham Lincoln biography for where he left off.

After an hour or so, Nathan asked Eugene if he wanted his coffee freshened. He did. Nathan took away the cups, the barista got off her stool and, when he returned to the table, said, "It's a shame Lincoln never got to write his memoirs."

"It's the most important book never written."

Nathan nodded, sipped his coffee.

They talked more the next morning. Nathan was twenty-nine. Never finished high school. He and his wife, Paulette, owned a home. She worked all day while he spent his afternoons and late nights renovating the house—knocking down walls, rewiring, laying tile. "She could be living someplace nicer if she'd have married a guy who could make a decent living like I told her."

Eugene looked at his watch. "You're getting a late start."

"One of my shifts ends when she gets home in the evening and the next one starts when she goes to sleep. Figuring out how to install a new wall plug sure beats lying there next to her wondering what in the hell this woman is doing with a guy like me."

"What does she do?" asked Eugene, his thumb holding his place in a book of Noel Coward plays. "Your wife?"

"She's an assistant curator at a museum. Serious business," said Nathan.

"Her coworkers love her sleeve tattoos, but I can't imagine what they think of me."

"What museum?"

"The Weisz, over on Hudson."

"I designed that museum."

"It's nice," said Nathan, closing a book on Klimt, opening one on Egon Schiele.

"You don't like it."

"I like it."

"But?"

"But nothing."

"Have you ever tried lying to Paulette?"

"No."

"Don't start."

"OK," said Nathan. "But." He closed the Schiele book, pulled an ancient toothpick from his shirt pocket, and popped it into the corner of his mouth. He chewed on the toothpick as though it contained whatever he was going to say next. "It's a little, I dunno, bloodless," he finally said. "A little, what's the word? Austere."

"Austere?"

"Paulette says she gets the feeling none of the rooms really want you in them."

Eugene had been smiling this whole time. When he realized that he did not, in fact, want someone to speak honestly on the subject of his life's work, the smile hung there but ceased to mean anything. Then it was gone. "And you've seen so much of the world that you get to be so certain of things?" he said, and was immediately embarrassed that he had.

Nathan hung his head and nodded slow. "No," he said, shrinking like a scolded child, "I probably haven't."

Pulling into the Barnes and Noble parking lot the next morning, Eugene worried that Nathan wasn't going to show. He had been vain and unpleasant and feared he had turned away the one person he enjoyed talking to in months. He was embarrassed. By his own reaction and with the knowledge that, no matter how old he might get, this was one of those lessons he'd never stop relearning and forgetting. That nobody really wants to hear the truth about himself.

But Nathan was there at his usual time and he sat with Eugene and they read and talked as if what happens one day has no bearing on the next. Eugene didn't ask for any more truth, and their conversations, for the next several weeks, remained rooted in books and home repairs and questions to which the answers were usually, "Yup."

One afternoon, a new snow covering the world outside, Eugene got up from their table and slid his arms into his coat. For no particular reason, he asked Nathan if he thought he could use a swim.

"I have a little time," said Nathan.

The lifeguard on duty at the natatorium shirtlessly chatted up the concessions girl. Children in class, adults at work, everyone else staying inside and warm, the pool, like the café, belonged to Eugene and Nathan. Eugene swam up and down the same lane he always used. Nathan, wearing only boxer shorts, wedged himself into a corner and paddled at the water with his legs. He looked so young. He had one of those faces that would always be young but tried to mask it by calculating every room he's in, even this one, with a furrowed detachment. Eugene finished his laps and joined Nathan in the shallow end.

"I never really learned to swim," said Nathan. "If they taught that in school, I wasn't there anymore by the time they got to it."

"You didn't like school," said Eugene, beginning his tai chi routine.

"Nah."

"Too hard?"

"Too poor. The other kids, they could tell I didn't belong. They could smell it. Literally. They called me Stink Boy. For ten years they called me that.

Stink Boy. I bathed. I washed my clothes." Nathan pressed his chin to his chest and smelled his left then his right shoulder. "How did I smell poor? Tell me that."

Eugene glided his body and limbs from maneuver to maneuver. He didn't know what any of them were called or even if they were referred to as maneuvers. Positions was more like it. But he liked *maneuvers*.

"It was just my mom and me," he went on. "She worked hard to send me to that school, but I couldn't do it. They used to throw balled-up sheets of paper at my head in class. I'd turn around and they'd be staring at the board, none of them even cracking a smile. Then the teacher would call me out for not paying attention. What does a fifteen-year-old kid do about that?"

Eugene thought about that for a minute and honestly didn't know.

"I think about that a lot," Nathan went on. "If we decide who we're going to be or if that's decided for us by stuff that happens."

"Something on your mind, Nathan?"

"Paulette and I," his voice went flat. "We've been fighting."

"For how long?"

"A year now."

"What would end it?"

"Having a baby."

Eugene had learned them, the maneuvers, by watching Nira in the pool every morning at dawn. He would sit off to the side in a glider, sipping coffee, pretending to read the *Financial Times*. "That's easy," Eugene said. "Have a baby."

It was hard for Eugene to imagine his pool and not see Nira's porcelain face, her hair up under a cap, her chin set upon the ledge. "It's so empty in here," she would say, her voice nearly swallowed by the cavernous ceiling. "Shouldn't we think about filling it with some little bodies? Some laughter?"

To which Eugene would say something evasive, but not too evasive. Soon. Next year. Once this next project wraps up. Something that made having children with this woman he loved so much seem inevitable, just not right now. Because, really, that's how Eugene felt about it. Inevitable. Not right now.

She'd roll her eyes at him and curl her lips into a snarl that was really a smile. "I'm holding you to that, Mister," she'd say, kicking herself away from the ledge and into a backstroke. "You'll see."

He hid from her how uneasy the subject made him. What he liked about buildings was how if he planned well enough, they'd stand forever. Or damn near. People were different. He'd seen up close how fragile they are. How thinly the human body clings to life. Green grass growing up around dead children. Women turned inside out. Stepping over so much man-made death as though it wasn't there. As though getting to the next place was all it took to leave it behind.

But he did try to get to that next place for her. And almost did. Twice. With the news of each pregnancy, Nira glowed like new light and he swore to himself that he would, when the time came, be as in love with those children as he was with her.

She lost the first child, a girl, after three months of pregnancy. Nira insisted on a proper funeral. At the cemetery, children were buried in a section called Babyland. Signs with arrows nailed to trees. *Babyland, this-a-way!* they seemed to say. Like a damn theme park, Eugene thought, walking with Nira to the small fresh-dug grave.

The second made it five months. Another girl. Nira barely survived. She was lucky, but there was damage and she would never have a child of her own. Maybe, the doctors said, if she had been younger.

"What if I don't love it?" said Nathan. "What if loving it isn't enough? What if, no matter what I do or how hard I work, kids throw wads of paper at its head in high school because it's not like them? Or worse, what if it is like them?"

Nira was still in the hospital when he returned to Babyland to bury the second child. What he felt more than anything that day was the lifting of a terrible weight. To Eugene, every life was a tragedy waiting to happen. The miscarriages and almost losing Nira only proved him right. That part of their lives was now past, and they still had each other. Which was more than he ever needed.

"What if all you wanted out of life was to make your wife happy?" he said to Nathan. "And when she's gone, and it's too late, you realize that's the one thing you never got around to."

Nathan sat down the next morning with a book of Edward Hopper paintings. Eugene tried not to think about that. Tried not to look. He read and reread the same paragraph from *Great Expectations* three times. "This was the first naked woman I ever saw," Nathan said. "For the life of me, I can't even remember the name of my first flesh-and-blood naked woman. But her." Nathan lifted the book and pointed to a nude woman sitting in an angle of sunlight. "I remember everything about her."

"She doesn't look very happy to be nude."

"That's not why she's unhappy," said Nathan. He laid the book flat. "What about you?"

"Why am I unhappy?"

"The first naked woman you ever saw."

"It's not a good story."

"Tell it anyway."

"When people ask you stories about wars or naked women, they want the stories to go a certain way. Mine's about both and I'm telling you that it won't go the way you want."

The way Nathan moved his eyebrows told Eugene to go on and tell it. So he did, starting with how he would always be the kind of man who saw men he shot writhe and die before he saw his first naked woman. How it didn't happen until he was twenty, late in life even then. It should have happened sooner, he knew, but there always seemed to be things that needed doing. More serious things. Work, school, then war. Sooner than alone on foot in the woods north of Aachen, crouched in brush, his M1 against his hip, watching three German women, girls really, floating and splashing in the River Wurm.

Nathan asked what was wrong with that story, and Eugene told him what was wrong with it were the parts he hadn't come to yet. Like what he knew and those girls didn't. What he and his company found in some shallows just a half mile upstream. Bodies, dozens of them, and pieces of bodies, chewed by bullets, shells, every damn thing. The bodies had been there for weeks, at least, sucking up water on one side and sun heat on the other, bloating, rotting, turning colors, turning the water colors. Sometimes Eugene went years without wondering which side eventually claimed those bodies and gave them a proper funeral. Sometimes hours. Not the men of Dog Company. He knew that and, for all he knew, they never were claimed. To this day, brown bones might jut from the Wurm, one more generation finding them easier to leave in the water than bury in the ground.

Two of the three German girls were blonde and could have been the same girl twice. The other, with red, straight hair, would dunk herself under, then rise up and, standing like a statue, shoot an angle of that human broth through her front two teeth and onto the blonde girls. They would laugh and so vividly Eugene remembered their laughter. How it was like music. How they were the most beautiful things he had ever seen.

And he remembered how easy it would have been to raise his rifle and put three rounds into the brains of those girls. For their unnatural joy in this place. Their oblivion to the horrors their fathers and brothers made Eugene travel halfway around the world to see and do. That they could be so covered in death and never have to know.

He unlocked his M1's safety and told himself that he would aim and fire in just a moment, just one more moment. And he was telling himself this when the girls got out, wrung damp their hair, dressed, and disappeared on bare feet through the mouth of a trail in the far bank's treeline.

"Those are the things that make you who you are," Eugene said after a long time, aware Nathan was looking at him, that his own eyes were focused on a knot in the table, and that neither one of them had blinked in quite a while. "Those are the things you don't tell your wife because you're afraid she won't love you anymore."

"I don't know, man," said Nathan. "They seem to find a way to love us anyways."

The Hopper book wasn't opened to Nira's painting. Not even to a major work. Just an empty room. One of Hopper's many empty rooms.

"I hope so."

Eugene drove home that night, leaving behind the hum of city, of traffic and the living. He switched on the kitchen light and fixed himself a sandwich. Everything he touched—the countertop, the plate, the knife he used to smear the mayo—was clean and cold.

He put the plate and the knife in the empty dishwasher, turned it on, and poured a glass of wine. To walk the house from end to end, setting foot in each room, took fifteen full minutes. After an hour of trying to settle on a spot to sit and drink his wine, Eugene found himself in the kitchen again and the wine the temperature of his hand.

The subject of children had been long since settled by doctors and then more doctors when he and Nira attended the black tie opening of the Weisz. The event was held in the museum's grand atrium, a wide-open space of cement and steel. Millionaires glad-handed, laughed, and smoked to the echoing harmony of a children's choir. Eugene held onto his glass of wine like a ripcord. He was uncomfortable at these parties no matter how often his line of work put him in them. His preferred tactic was to entrench himself in a corner with Nira while she whispered little jokes to him. But they became separated and Eugene found himself in the center of a circle of men he barely knew swamping him with hearty congratulations.

When he was finally able to extricate himself, he found Nira standing alone, watching the children's choir. He sidled up next to her and she gave no indication that she was aware of him. "They sound like angels," she said finally.

Eugene offered her some of his wine. She didn't want any. He asked her if she was all right.

"I was just thinking, watching all those suits slap you on the back and whatnot, you smiling, looking so proud, not knowing quite what to say." A song wound to a close. Before the next could begin, the room became suddenly and impossibly quiet. "I was just thinking—you never wanted children."

"No," Eugene said, thinking there was going to be more. Thinking Nira was working her way towards some question. But that was the question. And he had answered it so honestly and easily he surprised even himself. In a brutal, jagged world where everyone dies, there had been room in his heart for her and nothing after her. She was the last thing he could risk losing. He didn't know that when he asked her to marry him. Now they both knew, staring at other people's children, standing there like two strangers waiting for a bus. They drove home in silence.

The next morning, she was up before him. He got up and awkwardly made his way through the house not knowing how things were going to be between them. Coffee percolated in the kitchen, angles of sunlight cut through the rooms, and he found her in the middle of what she did every morning. Swimming. Before too long, what had always been their life, and what their life together would always be, became normal again.

Years later, Nira didn't have much time left when in the pool at dawn every morning became every other morning. When she didn't want to go in at all, Eugene knew it was the end. After the end, when Eugene learned what it was to live waiting for something that would never come, the house took on the feel of a mausoleum. Which must have been what it always was to her.

The worst part wasn't being alone. The worst part was not knowing if how much he loved her, or if the way he loved her, had been enough. He needed to know that it was. That even though Nira didn't get the life she wanted, she died happy with the one she got.

What he did know was that she would have been a wonderful mother. And instead of a child, he gave her this house. This house, he thought, gulping down the warm wine, standing in front of a window overlooking a lake he couldn't see. A window that might as well have been a black wall. This big, empty house.

*

Nathan walked into the Barnes and Noble and stood over Eugene. He didn't order coffee. He didn't unbutton his pea coat. "Let's go," he said, pointing outside with his thumb.

"Go where?"

"It's a surprise. Get your coat."

They drove in Nathan's '67 Mercury, heat blasting, through the old industrial district, burned-out and long-abandoned factories tombing the empty road. Dead barons built their mansions a little ways down, just far enough away from the smoke and noise that made their millions. Those old families were gone now, their big names forgotten, the money spent. But the mansions still stood, big and beaten, empty hulks of leaning pillars and broken glass. The mansions streamed by, Eugene turning his head from side to side to see them all, Nathan flicking ash out his cracked window.

"They were something once," said Eugene.

Nathan pulled the Mercury to a stop. He and Eugene crossed the road and stood before the mansion that didn't belong with the others. The one that was flat and angular. Though the wood was rotting and the cement was pocked and crumbling, it was, unmistakably, a Frank Lloyd Wright original.

"I come here sometimes," said Nathan. "Just to look."

"It's seen better days. That's for sure."

"So have you." They both laughed with only their breath, without making any real noise.

"Do you see that?" Eugene pointed off to the side of the house. Nathan craned his neck and squinted. "This was one of the first homes to have a garage. Cars didn't even go in reverse then. The garage floor was a turntable that spun the car back towards the road. I doubt it still does that."

"Hard to say what's left. About ten years ago it was subdivided into five apartments," Nathan said. "I wonder if they know what they're living in."

"There are a lot of houses like this." Eugene nudged with his foot a broken tricycle half-buried in the snow. "With histories that don't mean a damn thing to the people inside because life moves forward."

"The city's trying to put some money together to buy it. Turn it into a museum."

"You live in a museum like you take pictures at a funeral," said Eugene, burying his hands deep inside his pockets. He pointed towards the house with his chin. "I wonder where they'll go."

"Someplace else, I guess."

"What a waste."

Eugene did not want the house that he had built for Nira—the house she never asked for—to be waiting for him at the end of the day. He did not want to go there ever again, seeing in it—in every wall, every room, every slab of marble and bend of iron—a man who married a woman and then never figured out how to love one more thing that could die.

"I work on our house the way I would if I was fixing up a place like this." Nathan lit a new cigarette on the remains of the last. "I'm doing what I can to make it the home she deserves."

Eugene's chest felt empty. He breathed in deep but couldn't find enough oxygen to fill it. "That's going to take doing more than what you're doing now."

"I know," Nathan said. "We'll see."

They left a few minutes later. We'll see, Eugene repeated to himself, knowing that he was out of those. We'll sees.

Paulette walked out of their bathroom, the reds and purples and the blue lines of her sleeve tattoos—the blurred swirling of naked women and playing cards and skulls and Latin phrases—popping against the white of her skin and the black of her dress. She held up a thin cardigan and asked Nathan, "Sleeves or no sleeves?"

"He was an art lover," Nathan said, slipping his blazer over a white, short-sleeve button down.

She dropped the cardigan to the floor and smiled. "Sleeves then," she said.

Eugene didn't show at Barnes and Noble one morning. A few days later, Nathan read some very nice articles about Eugene's life. He died at home.

"Peacefully," the obituary read, and Nathan hoped that was true.

Nathan helped Paulette into the passenger's seat of the '67 Mercury, and by the time he was around the car and behind the steering wheel, she had her arms wrapped around her stomach as though she were fine but the six months of baby inside might be chilly. She looked so fragile sitting there, round softness strapped in and surrounded by all of that exposed metal and hard angles of the door and dash. Nathan drove uneasy, below the speed limit, taking turns as though the driveshaft were glass. A man was coming by the next day to kick the tires and make an offer, and even that was too far away.

They arrived late at the St. Peter in Chains Cathedral and Nathan circled several times, looking for a spot that was not too far for Paulette to walk. "If anyone asks, tell them I'm retarded," he said, pulling into a handicapped space by the front entrance. He said this, cut the motor, and made no indication that he was ever going to leave the car.

"Keep making that face and it won't be a problem," said Paulette, but he didn't really hear her. Just like he wasn't really looking at the fat, gray bricks that made the St. Peter in Chains or the two ushers smoking by the front entrance or anything at all.

"Hmm?" he said.

She reached out to him and smoothed down the side of his Brylcreemed hair and asked him if he was sad. He was sad, but not right then. He was thinking about whether those who knew Eugene Meridian would be asked to say a few words. And, if so, would he? There was plenty to say about a man who fought a war and did his best to worship a woman he adored and worked like a man who knew what work was and built buildings that would remain standing long after every person walking the earth today was dead.

But surely everyone there would already know this. What they couldn't know was that Eugene was also a man willing to give the last months of his life to an unemployed high school dropout who had no idea how in the hell he was going to become the man he needed to become for both his wife and unborn baby. How could he explain to a room full of strangers that he found it comforting that a man like Eugene could live a life like the one he lived and die certain of nothing but his own failures?

"I'm not sad," Nathan said. "I'm just nervous, is all."

Comforting because it meant maybe there was more to the sum total of a man's life than what he sees when he looks back. Nathan knew he would never feel worthy of what his life was asking of him but, goddamn, he was going to try. And if a lifetime of trying left Nathan with nothing but the gnaw of regret, maybe he'd be wrong too.

How could he explain that? And why would they care?

NUCLEAR SUMMER

My son Johnny had a couple good grabs at first. Malcolm's son Beau pitched three innings of one-hit, one-run ball. Toby didn't have a son or any children or a wife but thought that appearing at sporting events was sort of expected of him as the mayor of Great Bend Township. It got a little hairy there at the end when one of the boys lost the strike zone, but the Cardinals bested the Padres 4-3, the teams *good-gamed* each other across the diamond, everyone played fair and got good exercise, and then it was time for ice cream.

The three of us—Malcolm, Toby, and I—sat on cement benches that arced around a cement table in front of the McDonald's shaped-like-a-house, eating the vanilla soft-serve it took ten minutes to get and smoking the cigarettes we already had.

"My wife hates things shaped like other things," I said. "Staplers shaped like little animals. Hats shaped like food."

"You know what else she hates, partner?" said Malcolm. He called everyone partner. "You."

"It's not that she doesn't love me. She just loves this other guy a lot more."

"Buck and Lizzie aren't married anymore, and Great Bend has a McDonald's," Toby said. "This has not been my most effective term."

As mayor, Toby felt responsible for the McDonald's. More specifically, he worried that the voters were going to hold him responsible. No one wanted it, including him, yet here it was. The whole affair, he often said, was a real blow to his credibility. Still, he'd eaten dinner there almost every night since it opened the previous April. It's a mystery what he thought that did to his credibility.

"Christ, Toby," I said. "Does anyone even run against you?"

To preserve the local economy, Toby passed a law declaring that no chains could open in Great Bend as long as they looked like chains. McDonald's skirted the intent of Toby's law by building a McDonald's shaped-like-a-house. Window panes. Wood siding painted cream. Maroon shutters and gutters to match. Even a damn welcome mat. Toby leaned back, shook his head slow, and balanced his cone on his belly. "*The Great Bend Bugler* isn't going to forget a thing like this."

"You know why they call 'em chains, don't ya'?" Malcolm smoked Winchesters, those little cigars with the white plastic filters. Between the cowboy hat he always wore, his blonde mustache, and furrowed brow, he could have been one of the cowboys in the Winchester ads. "The more you've got, the heavier you get."

"I love it when you get all folksy and homespun," said Toby. "You're from Seattle."

"Yeah, *west* Seattle."

Malcolm invested himself in fatherhood like nothing I'd ever seen. His dad flew an F-4B Phantom II in Vietnam that never found its way back. Malcolm said his father existed for him as a series of images—a gray terry-cloth bathrobe behind a snapping newspaper, a cold leather jacket hugging him goodbye before dawn—but he could piece the images together into a living memory the way you can read in dreams. Individual words that never become coherent ideas. Malcolm swore that his son would know, if nothing else, him.

He said to me once that there was nothing he wouldn't burn to the ground if it came between him and Beau. That kind of parenting seemed a little excessive to me. I told him I approved of the sentiment and all, but I never found raising a son or doing anything else in Great Bend to require that kind of deliberate energy. Malcolm said that kind of thinking was probably why Lizzie left.

Cardinals and Padres and parents buzzed around the patio, a line of them snaking from the registers all the way out the doors. Johnny, Beau, and a few of the other boys, their cleats tied over the shoulders, their red stirrups slacked behind their heels, stood in the parking lot gazing at a Jaguar XJR-S7. We were all in shadow, but the low-hanging sun made a golden awning over our heads. Above that, the sky was a clear, cobalt blue. That stars would be out in less than an hour seemed insane.

"Did you hear about Mr. Church over at the Acme?" I said, pointing with my head to the Acme on the other side of the parking lot.

"He die?"

"Canned."

"Canned?" said Toby. "For what? That man had a rare gift."

"He bagged and weighed produce and talked about the time he met Dwight Eisenhower until you walked away," said Malcolm.

"A rare gift," said Toby, nodding.

"They don't need him anymore. Got rid of the scales, too. They're putting these little numbered stickers on the fruits and vegetables. All the checkout girl has to do is type in the number and it tells her how much it is."

"When they get rid of the checkout girls is when I'll start worrying." Malcolm shot blue smoke out of his nostrils. "He's been drawing a pension for years. He only started working at the Acme 'cause he was bored after Mrs. Church died."

"Well, then," said Toby. "That makes it worse, doesn't it?"

"Hey, Buck. You ever wish Lizzie were dead? Or that Johnny didn't look so much like her?"

Lizzie was on her way to pick up Johnny. He spends the weekends in

Mogadore with her and this other guy, and I pretend like it all matters so little to me that I can't even remember this other guy's name. I wondered if he was going to be in the car with her. Or if she was going to kiss me goodbye. She would if she'd ever loved me.

"Yes," I said.

McDonald's designers had outmaneuvered Toby's zoning guidelines around the same time Lizzie left. Toby had been sitting in a lawn chair in his garage watching through binoculars the neighbors he didn't trust, and Malcolm was watering his yard in his cowboy hat and no shirt when Lizzie decided it was time for the figurative dissolution of our marriage to become ugly and public. After stuffing her purse full of underthings and a bottle of shampoo, she shot out the front door, yelling about how I was a ghost of a man. A vapor. And when you finally meet your rock, there's no going back.

"Why are you shouting?" I asked.

"Because if I wasn't," she said, each word louder than the one before, "you won't know when I'm gone!"

An accelerating Honda Accord makes a distinct sound. A gentle whine. Kinda like it's saying *Mmmeeeee*. That sound disappeared in the distance, and I was left staring at the exhaust cloud marking where Lizzie had just been. I was calm. Man, was I calm. I wasn't happy to see her go, but it was already done. Malcolm and Toby didn't need to know how hard it was going to be for me to live, so when they started clapping, I doffed an invisible cap and took a bow.

"I miss Lizzie," said Toby. "She was spry. Wasn't she just so spry?"

"She'll be here soon. You can tell her how spry she is then."

"I bet coming back here once a week just breaks her heart."

If they knew how much talking about Lizzie bothered me, it would stop. But there's no dignity to a ruined life. And that was about all I had left of our life together. A house and a yard and a dental practice covered with dignity. "I bet it doesn't," I said, leaning forward, planting my elbows on my knees, bracing myself for the conversation to be like this for a while. It would never stop.

"I bet every time she comes back to Great Bend she sees something that isn't the way it used to be," said Toby. "She's in a unique position to notice that kind of stuff."

"Leaving with the accelerator all the way down sure is a strange way to show your love for something. But if that's the case, Buck, maybe she isn't full of shit when she says she still loves you."

"Well, she moved here for a reason, didn't she? So did you." Toby pointed at Malcolm. "So did you." He pointed at me. "And I bet it wasn't because you all hoped to wake up one day and realize you're living in a Great Bend theme park?"

"Change is neither good nor bad, partner. It's just a thing that is." Malcolm had not been looking at Toby this whole time. He was looking through him, at Beau and Johnny and the other boys ogling the Jaguar XJR-S7. "We should worry about it the way a coffee table should worry about a knock at the door."

I was only half paying attention myself. Lizzie was going to arrive any second, and I had a lot riding on what happened after that. Last week, when I picked up Johnny at her new house in Mogodore, she didn't kiss me goodbye. We always kissed each other goodbye. During the divorce. After the divorce. Even when this other guy was in the room. It didn't look like it meant anything, but it did. Sure, he'd won. He was her rock and I got crushed. But she and I had some good years and a great kid together and twice a week, despite everything, we took the time to remind each other that that still meant something.

The only two times kissing goodbye wasn't muscle memory since our first date were the day she left and last week. I was standing in her and this guy's foyer, hands in my pockets, waiting for her to initiate. Johnny was in the car. "Well, that's about it," she said a few times, and I said, "Yep, yep." Waiting. Waiting. When I finally initiated, she radiated surprise like heat waves, like we hadn't been saying goodbye that way for thirteen years. But she did give me her cheek. Then this look, like when a teenage son asks his mother to sing him to sleep. Like, wasn't I a little old for that?

What made losing her in the first place any amount of okay was my belief that some things could never be lost utterly. But if I didn't kiss her that night, and if she didn't kiss me, it would mean she was lost, along with how I thought I'd always remember us.

Malcolm continued gazing off into the middle distance. Whatever was on his mind, I knew him well enough to know it had to do with something he saw on the news. With shaky, handheld footage of body-strewn fields—some new crop of unexplainable man-made dead—and how his concerns were in this whole other place, far above the likes of me and Toby.

"Remember those duck-and-cover movies they used to show us?" he finally said. "A bunch of kids our age are sitting in a classroom when a mushroom cloud blooms outside the window. They huddle under their desks, all calm, like they'll be dusting themselves off in just a minute or two and going on with the business of being kids. And alive." He said all this without looking away from the boys, the Winchester filter clicking between his teeth. "I think about that and I think about what lunacy our kids are gonna find perfectly normal because they trust us."

"You know, Beau looked good out there today. Some real snap on some of those curves," Toby said. Under the right circumstances, he could have been a truly excellent politician. Then he said to me, "Don't get me wrong, Buckeye. Johnny handles a fine first base. But, you know, he'll probably quit here in a few years. Being so much like his mother and all."

It would never stop.

Mmmeeeee. Lizzie's Honda Accord pulled into the McDonald's parking lot. I stubbed my cigarette out in my ice cream and tossed the cone over my shoulder. "Ladies," I said, hoisting myself off the bench and into the parking lot to see what the last thirteen years of my life had amounted to. Not the sort of walk you want to take in flip-flops.

"Gets gas mileage for crap," one of the boys was saying about the Jaguar when I entered earshot. It wasn't Johnny who said it, and I wondered if he had any opinions whatsoever on gas mileage. Or if he was old enough for his opinions to count as opinions.

He and his teammates did this handshake, high-five combination and we walked to Lizzie's car. She was parked. Instead of getting out, saying hello to the old neighbors, maybe kicking back with some soft-serve under a hell-of-a-nice setting sun, she looked like she did when the gas station attendant was taking his sweet time with her change. Checking her face in the rearview mirror from the right side, then the left. Smiling like a crazy person while picking her teeth with her pinky nail. Flipping through mail she'd already flipped through. But she was alone.

Johnny got in on the passenger side. I leaned against the driver-side door, my arms folded atop the window track, my head in the car. If Lizzie didn't kiss me, it would not be for lack of opportunity.

"Is it a McDonald's or is it grandmother's house?" she said. "What does it say about a society that it produces dishonest buildings?" She leaned over in her seat and kissed Johnny on the forehead. "Hey, kid."

"Then again," I said, "aren't all McDonald's lying about being restaurants?" When she straightened up again, she was so close to me I could smell her makeup. Nothing. "You missed it. Our man had a heck of a game."

"Did he? Did your dad tell you that you had a heck of a game?"

"No," Johnny said.

"What? Of course I did."

"Buck."

"I did."

"Buck." The second time she said my name there was, in her voice, the gleam of fresh pity.

"Well, I said it in the way things are understood between fathers and sons."

"Do you really want me to ask Johnny if it's his fault that his father didn't tell him he played a good game?"

"This conversation is not going the way I thought it would."

"And I know that's a very difficult thing for you." She put her sunglasses on. It was suddenly like talking to her through an air vent. "Buck, it's fine. Really."

"What's fine?"

"You."

"I'm fine? Thanks." She wasn't being snarky or snide. She wasn't being anything. She just really wanted me to know that me being who I am was OK with her. "I always wanted to be fine."

"Do you remember who you were before you were fine? Before this place?"

"Like I am now? Only less?"

"Somewhere along the line you got it in your head that doing nothing wasn't destructive."

"If everything's good the way it is, you leave it alone," I said. "Isn't that what you do?"

"No. That's what *you* do."

I looked from her to Johnny. Back again. They were so much alike. Never more than right then. Sharp, elfin features, like they should have been off causing trouble for us mortals in some Shakespearean dell. Two versions of the same face seeing the ways I was different now, the ways I wasn't who I used to be. They could see it. I couldn't. I looked at my reflections in Lizzie's sunglasses. There were two of me floating there and I just couldn't see it. Still living in our town, in our house, still wearing my ring, I was right there. All this time, I would have sworn that I was more right there than any of us.

"And you were supposed to hate things shaped like other things. I guess that was before you found your rock," I said, knowing I would never again be so close to her and have to wonder how it was going to end. "Your rock shaped-like-a-man."

Lizzie smiled, but it was only a movement of her mouth, an acknowledgment that, yes, I had in fact said something. "Living with a man shaped like the man I married was worse."

If I was right there and had been all this time, when did she start talking to me like she was talking about me at my funeral? Like I was a decent man who died a dull, easy-to-comprehend death, and life moves forward. Why didn't I try to stop her when she left? Why didn't I try to talk her out of it? Swear to change and mean it? But it wasn't until now that I realized that losing her, and I mean really losing her, was even possible. And it had happened so long ago.

I stepped away from the car. She backed out. They pulled away, past the McDonald's, down the street. Taillights. Gone. And from the patio, from anywhere, I just looked like a man waving goodbye. Goodbye, now. Not a man who'd lost everything he loved. Because what does that look like?

"This Halabja thing has me, I dunno." Malcolm was talking about genocide when I got back to my seat, and Toby was barely listening. "Five thousand dead, and counting. You guys see this?"

"Yes," I said.

"Nope," said Toby.

"Sarin. That's what they're saying was used."

"Spock's dad?" Toby joked.

"Buck, a dentist is sorta like a doctor. What do you know about Sarin?"

He already knew. There wasn't anything that could kill entire neighborhoods at a time that Malcolm couldn't talk about, or listen to, for hours. It made him feel better knowing his fears could be put into words. Made tangible. Clouds of death. Jack-booted thugs. Wars eating fathers and sons like great-bellied monsters.

"There are these chemicals in your body that make your muscles and glands do stuff." I lit a cigarette, aware of the irony. "Or not do stuff. Sarin makes those chemicals go crazy. Uncontrolled drooling, sweating, shitting, pissing, vomiting, laughing."

"Is it the weekend already?" When neither of us laughed, Toby retreated back into his ice cream.

"Or paralysis. Everything inside you just locks up. You're dead, but you're not. Well, until you are. Because that's another thing Sarin does. It finally gets around to killing you."

"They keep finding these villages where it looks like the earth just stopped moving. Dead children stroking dead cats. Dead mothers washing dead babies," said Malcolm. "Like God pressed pause. Only it wasn't God."

"Sarin, huh? Sounds like nasty business." Toby twisted in his seat, looking for a polite place to flick his cigarette ash. "Let me guess. It's the kind of stuff that when it gets on you, water makes it worse."

"It doesn't really get on you," I said. "It's a vapor. It gets *in* you."

"If that's how a thing starts, how's it gonna end?"

"That's what I've been saying," said Toby, remembering where he was, that there was no reason for him to politely dispose of his ash, that he would use that McDonald's to stub out a cigarette the size of a water tower if he had one. "What's Great Bend gonna lose next?"

"I don't worry about the turning," said Malcolm. "I worry about the turning into. Not the ticking, but the blast."

Malcolm believed there was only this one world any one of us knew enough about to prepare our sons to live in. He was afraid our sons were never going to live in that world. He was right to be afraid. They weren't. Where he was wrong was thinking our world was going to end in devastation. In flash and fire. In his nightmares, he saw Beau, his skin leathering under desert sun, clutching a Kalashnikov he took from a man he killed with his own hands.

I didn't have the heart to tell Malcolm that the ticking *was* the blast. The world he was so afraid of losing was already gone. Long gone. It disappeared one imperceptible mutilation at a time. Something was lost and no one noticed. Then something else. Then something else. Before you knew it, your wife was never going to kiss you again. Before you knew it, you were eating ice cream in a McDonald's shaped-like-a-house, in a town shaped-like-your-town.

"Fucking barbarians," Malcolm said, cracking his knuckles, finger by finger. "Killing their own like that."

I thought about Mr. Church and how he was going to die without that job to go to. How Toby had it right, just too late. And how being right too late was the same as being wrong forever. He crushed out his cigarette beneath a sockless leather loafer and lit another. Some parents and their kids hung around, but we'd be the last ones to leave. We always were. The sun gone, we could barely see the ash swirling at our feet. Doing very little, we had really made a mess of things.

GOD BLESS YOUR
CROOKED LITTLE HEART

Brandon and Emmavail drove south, the San Diego skyline long gone, Tijuana, burritos the size of human heads, Tecate rivers, and the Mexican techno trio Tres, Tres Jugadores, just beyond the vanishing point of Highway 5. Brandon, behind mirrored sunglasses, organized and filed in his mind the funny stories from the week he hadn't yet told Emmavail. He looked at her, gray tank top almost flaunting the raspberry, Kentucky-shaped scar splashed across her shoulder blade and forearm.

"It's your turn." There was an open dictionary in her lap. "Ask Webster a question."

Will my girlfriend slap me across the head and call me a sap if I asked her to marry me, he wanted to know. Will my girlfriend shrug and say, "Them's the breaks," if she finds a man more clever and cool than me?

"When we look back on this trip to the happiest place on earth, what will we remember?"

Emmavail closed her eyes, arced her head skyward and flipped through the pages chanting, "tellmewhentostoptellmewhentostoptellmewhentostop."

"Stop."

Slouched over the dictionary, index finger pressed to page, "Argonaut," she said. "One. Any band of heroes sailing with Jason in quest of the Golden Fleece. Two. An adventurer engaged in a quest."

"Expectations."

"No shitsky." She cracked the window and lit a cigarette. "I'm not feeling epic at all."

"What are you feeling?"

"That's a boring question. Try again."

Stuck behind a Nissan Stanza and thirteen other cars snaking through the border crossing, Emmavail playing swami, they asked *Merriam-Webster's Collegiate Dictionary: Eleventh Edition* questions like, "What did my first grade teacher think of me?" "Why am I afraid of pictures of the Titanic?" "What's the most disgusting thing I've ever accidentally eaten?"

"Infrequent."

"Thymine."

"Portugal."

When the man in the booth asked them if they had anything to declare, Brandon told him, "*Me temo que mi novia y yo no tengo la misma definición de amor.*" The man called Brandon a schmuck and waved them through.

"What did you say to him?" asked Emmavail, setting Webster down at her feet.

"I told him that if there's a Golden Fleece somewhere around here, me and this girl here are gonna find it."

Crossing the Rio Tijuana, Emmavail removed the sunglasses from Brandon's face and put them on herself. "Brando," she said, smiling, Brandon looking into his own convex reflection, "you are a schmuck."

They drove to the north end of Zona Centro and checked into the Hotel Nelson. Emmavail tried finagling a discount by telling the woman at the desk they were newlyweds. The woman at the desk snorted. They showered and changed and set out on foot to Revolución, half the sky a deepening blue, half the color of sangria, through air thick with sizzling meat and phosphorous.

They held hands as they walked. To Brandon, there was sex in most everything Emmavail did. Over the previous year and a half, he often found himself looking at her and thinking thoughts like: What I wouldn't give to be that box of Frosted Mini-Wheats. What I wouldn't give to be that copy of *National Geographic*. She was chain-smoking, loosing cigarettes from the pack with her one free hand, lighting the fresh with the cached, and it was driving Brandon the good kind of crazy.

He wanted to tell her how happy he was right then. He wanted to tell her that it was a miracle that there could be these minutes amid these days where two people got to be so happy, given all of the people who had lived and would live long lives and never know this kind of happy. So why shouldn't they give some thought to maybe making this miracle permanent? Seriously, he'd say. Why not get married? Why not be the people who make the conscious choice to be happy and alive and young all on the same day?

Especially if she was going to insist on being so close to him that he could turn his head and see her face lit by some other country's night magic, smoking her cigarettes like only she could, making Brandon wish he was dangling from her lips and on fire.

Hell, given all that, not marrying someone who loves you that much would be cruel and stupid.

But Brandon knew how she felt about the sort of man who said things like that. The way she made him feel, she had made many men feel before. And each one told her all about these new feelings she gave him, thinking it would be just that sort of honesty that would make him different from the men who came before. "What they were trying to do was validate me," she told Brandon once, early on in their relationship, "for having the fortitude to be who I was for all that time it took me to finally meet and complete them."

Keeping Emmavail meant—had always meant—keeping who he really was and what he really wanted to tell her to himself. "The beasts," he told her then.

"What's going on in that head of yours?" she asked, flicking a cigarette she'd smoked down to the cotton onto the confetti and puke-strewn sidewalk before them.

"They say that kissing a smoker is the same as licking an ashtray," he said. "Given the choice, I'm here to tell you that I'd pick you over an ashtray any day of the week."

At Cabeza de Vaca's, they ordered burritos, guacamole, and margaritas and sat at a lacquered wood table that might have at one time been a door. The burritos, as advertised, were in fact the size of human heads, and Brandon ate half of his. Emmavail, all of a hundred pounds, ate like a cowboy and finished hers as well as her third margarita and asked Brandon if he was going to make that face when he danced tonight.

"What face?"

"That face you make." She closed her eyes, slacked open her mouth, and bobbed her head back and forth. "Like you're waiting for someone to kiss you."

She liked pointing out to Brandon the ways in which he was not cool. It was his own fault, he knew, that he didn't give as good as he got. Like telling her that she said reactionary when she means reactive or that she farted like his grandfather. It was his own fault that, instead, he would laugh as if Brandon were some fool they both knew.

He picked up the half-eaten burrito and worked the tortilla casing like the jaws of a puppet. "Eef I make thawt face," the burrito said in a French accent, "I don't do eet on purpose."

Tecate and tequila made their movement from bar to bar into a flipbook with pages missing. Brandon could remember leaving Cabeza de Vaca's but not the walk to a place called Manico Panico. He could remember ordering six Margarita Heyworths, but not how many he finished himself or paying or leaving. He could remember giving the man at the door their tickets and telling Emmavail that this was what being alive was like, but not what she said to that. "Focus. Focus," he said to himself, slapping and not feeling his face.

Tres, Tres Jugadores took the stage just before midnight with a track from their new album. Sweating, holding his fist in the air, Brandon stepped back to watch Emmavail slink and sway to the baselines reverberating through their bodies like wind through shadows, a cigarette dangling from her lips. Five feet on a dance floor can be another time zone. Emmavail was so surrounded by men who thought they were dancing with her, there were times he couldn't see her. When he could, the men were leaning in close, whispering things that made her laugh from her belly.

She finally cut through the men and closed the space between them. He wanted her to say something about all of these douchebags. How forward men made her feel like fish food. How these shows used to be so much better before Tres, Tres Jugadores started blowing up. She slid up to him, pelvis to pelvis, and whispered, "Brando, you're doing it."

"Doing what?"

She bounced her head and gaped her mouth. "The face."

"Deal with it," he said.

Goddammit, he thought. Goddammit, goddammit, goddammit.

Brandon woke up naked in their bed at the Hotel Nelson in a tangle of white sheet, a naked Emmavail's back pressed to his front, fragments of sex had in his head. Yells and firecracker pops echoed from the street below, orange city glow smoldering the dark room, and he thought of when she first came into his life. How he had judged Emmavail without really knowing anything about her. She was a friend of a friend, and he heard her name a lot. People seemed to like saying it. He and Emmavail were at the same parties sometimes and, from afar, she struck him as both an obsolete beauty—maybe a flapper born a century late—and the kind of girl who knows what she looks like. With a name and face like that, Brandon assumed she was the kind of awful inside for which there are no negative repercussions. And he was disappointed in himself for thinking about her more than twice.

She heard he was a blood technician for the special effect firm *Danger,*

Will Robinson. Emmavail explained this over the phone when she invited him over to her apartment to help her with a Halloween costume. He agreed, hoping this girl would prove him right—that she was some combination of rotten, vapid, stupid, mean—so he could exorcise her from his mind.

Emmavail's idea was to dress up as a prom queen who gave herself a Cesarean. She already had the gown and the crown. Brandon brought the blood, a prosthetic baby, and twenty feet of sausage casing wrapped in white butcher paper. "Are those guts or umbilical?" she asked.

"Both."

She made him laugh and he made her grotesque. Brandon split Emmavail's gown from sternum to pelvis. He packed the sausage casing within the slit, fastening the greasy coils in place with piano wire so they'd bulge but not slop to the floor. He painted the new guts bloody with a barbeque brush and dripped long rivulets down the skirt front. With the last three feet of casing, he attached one end to Emmavail's gaping maw and the other to the prosthetic baby.

Standing before a floor-length mirror, Emmavail held her baby to her chest with one hand and slid the other over her slick insides. She moved slow, dreamy, like a girl practicing her *I dos.* "You pulverized me," she said.

"I wasn't the first." He had not seen the scar before or known that she was the kind of person who knew what surviving something was like. "What happened?"

"Oh, that." She turned towards Brandon, pressing her chin to her shoulder, but without actually looking at him. "Something I couldn't control happened to me this one time."

"What I fake, you've got for real."

She turned back to her reflection, to her toy blood, toy baby, toy brutality. "You fake it good."

I fake it good, he thought, lying next to her in bed, tracing the perimeter of her burn scar, wondering if the jerry-rigged skin was more or less sensitive than the rest of her body. Her mother had set her on fire when she was a baby. There was a court case she didn't remember, no father to speak of, and was raised by an aunt. That's all he knew. That's all she would tell him. She might have told him more, he thought, if he too had a scar. If they had in common something drastic and ghastly. A slit throat. A bullet wound. Or a past worth keeping secret. But his body held no stories, and he had been raised in a home that smelled like cinnamon by parents who lived and would die in Ohio. Parents who, when the Buckeyes play the Wolverines, make crab dip for their friends.

He thought about waking her, asking her if they really were in on this thing together. What he did instead was bury his face in the fine hairs on the back of her neck, close his eyes, and wonder what her answer might be. So long as the question stayed in his head, her answer might be yes. And he might believe her.

Emmavail shoplifted the way other women took long baths. She said it centered her. It was her alone time. The next morning, waiting for her to get back, it was Brandon's alone time too. The sun oppressive, the air like a fever, he sat on a bench between his car and the Hotel Nelson, staring at Tijuana in the light of day. It was like watching a marionette show when the light hits the stage just so, and you can see all of the strings. Everything is fake, hollow, and nothing, nothing is possible.

This isn't what the-rest-of-your-life love feels like, he thought. In a world without magic, his mind had nowhere else to go. He didn't know what that kind of love did feel like. Only that this wasn't it.

What sounded like midgets at a strip club—helium-tinged whoops and cackles—took Brandon out of his own head. Three Mexicans boys, brothers or close enough to brothers—prepubescent dough in neon T-shirts—had a dog surrounded. One of the boys spun lassos of clear liquid from a square can onto the dog. Another fumbled with a book of matches. "Hot dog!" chanted the third. "Hot dog!"

"Hey!" Brandon rose and headed for the boys. The dog, a woolly, bone-jagged stray, circled weakly, looking for a way out, finding only shins and thick-tongued tennis shoes two sizes too big. "Hey!" he said again.

Punching a ten-year-old in the face was a lot like how Brandon imagined it would be to punch a seal. Bone wrapped in spongy rubber. He'd never really punched anything living before but could punch that all day. The boy with the matchbook took the hit and then three drunken steps backwards before falling hard on his butt. Brandon grabbed a fistful of Hot Dog's T-shirt collar. Hot Dog took off, leaving the shirt empty in Brandon's hand like the result of a magic trick. He groped the air for the nearest ten-year old, but even Matchbook was out of reach, on his feet and gone. In one last gesture of fuck you, Brandon threw the shirt at the boys' backs shrinking down the street.

Just him and the dog then, Brandon leaned forward, his hands on his knees, breathing hard. They had dropped the matches. They'd find more, he knew. Or a lighter. Or two sticks to rub together. For sure, so long as they still had the lighter fluid, some other dog was screwed. Not this one, though, Brandon thought. The dog shook its coat, spuming the air with filth and naphtha. Still glistening, the rising sun itself seemed like it might be enough to explode the street creature.

"All right," said Brandon. "Let's go."

The dog stayed close. Brandon bought a bottle of water, got down on one knee, upended the bottle, and tried to get the dog as cleaned off as he could without actually touching it—him, he noticed, when the dog sat down on its rump. The water beaded and slid off the grimy coat onto the sidewalk. Brandon didn't know if he was doing any good whatsoever, but the dog was looking into his face—smiling—with a pure and stupid love.

Not many people were out and about. But enough so that every unattended animal shouldn't run the risk of combustion at the hands of children. Brandon seemed to be the only one who had noticed what almost happened. Or that three boys were assaulted by a twenty-five year old gringo, a gringo who then showered a dog with a water bottle. Not that he felt magnanimous. Not that he felt as though he had really done anything at all. Out of water, the dog was still a panting hand grenade. Even if he wasn't going to burn to death that way, the dog's gray coat was a patchwork of greasy clumps hanging like dreads and bare skin blistering in the blasting light. He was going to die out here, and it was going to be slow instead of fast. That's all he really did.

But, other than the mange and the black and crunchy gunk dripping from his eyes like melted wax and the worm-ridden heart and the stink of garbage emanating like heat waves, he really was a very well-put-together dog. Handsome, in his own way. The kind of dog that would fit in a trunk.

"I can't do it, guy."

He couldn't do it because Brandon had this idea in his head of who Emmavail had been dating for a year and a half. This guy, he didn't want to cry every time he saw a homeless person because of an episode of *Highway to Heaven* he saw as a boy where this homeless retarded kid had to shoplift cat food to feed his cat. He wasn't jealous when Emmavail danced with other men. He wasn't a sentimental fuck who felt morally obligated to dogs he saved from hellish deaths. Brandon wasn't this guy. He faked it good, but he didn't have the strength to fake it forever.

She'll figure it out, he thought. Tomorrow, maybe. The day after. Their thirtieth anniversary. And when she does, he can go ahead and consider his heart broken. Abandoning this dog was only postponing the inevitable. For both of them.

He looked from the dog to the street, a desolate canyon of closed storefronts and sun-bleached pavement, white tourists in khaki shorts and Panama hats drifting by, and no Emmavail. Then back to the dog. A pure and stupid love.

"Fuck it."

They walked back to the car. Along the way, Brandon bought a Styrofoam bowl full of beef and another bottled water. The dog finished the meat. Brandon filled and refilled the bowl with water, the dog lapping like a maniac.

When the bottle was empty, Brandon opened the trunk, moved their suitcase to the backseat, walked back to the trunk, and told the dog to jump in.

Idling in the mile-long queue filtering through the border crossing back into California, Brandon cranked the AC and the new Tres, Tres Jugadores album, hoping the sound would drown out any mysterious bumps or barks and that some of that cool air might make its way into the trunk. A dead dog, he figured, being harder to explain than a live one.

"What's that smell?" Emmavail reclined her seat and draped her leg out the window, her eyes hidden behind Brandon's sunglasses. They hadn't spoken since she returned to the car.

"What smell?"

"Like, like a broken Zippo."

"That is, I'm sure, nothing."

"Nothing?"

"Nothing. I'm sure. You're crazy."

"OK." She pulled a Parliament from the pack with her teeth. "I'm crazy."

"Um, could you maybe not smoke that?"

"Why not? If you're so sure it's nothing."

Because I don't want my trunk to blow up, he thought.

"I would just consider it a personal favor to me if you did not smoke that right now."

"My hero." She tossed the pack onto the dashboard.

They weren't moving. They weren't talking. Not too far ahead stood bored men with guns. Compared to that, the fact that Emmavail was bored could not have mattered less. He resented the huge swaths of time when he thought keeping her happy was all that mattered. How all of that time could have been put to better uses. Like learning the piano. Or buying a TV for each of his video game platforms and setting them up, side-by-side in his living room, like he always meant to do.

"All I know about my mom," Emmavail finally said, turning down the volume, "is that she was crazy. I don't know enough about her to know if I'm like her and that scares me. That's why I keep things from you. What's your excuse?" She turned away, staring out the window, then back at Brandon. "Are you hearing me, Brando?"

He was not hearing her. Only a fraction of him even knew she was talking, the rest of him focused on two things. How this was a bad planet if the destinies of two living things—if not man and woman, then man and dog—could never converge. And Mexican prison. In that order.

They pulled up to the booth and Emmavail's demeanor cleared. She turned the music back up, swaying her head, snapping her fingers. Brandon, sweating, dread coiled in his stomach, rehearsed the sentence, "No, sir, not a thing. No, sir, not a thing," in his mind.

"Do you have anything to declare?" asked the man in the booth.

"Tres, Tres Jugadores fucking rules," said Emmavail.

The man looked from Emmavail to Brandon. Brandon shrugged.

"It's true," he said. "They do."

The man waved them through, and Emmavail blew him a kiss.

Traffic thinned several miles up Highway 5. Brandon looked for a good spot to pull over and show Emmavail that he was the kind of person who sometimes smuggles dogs through border checkpoints and that she could take it or leave it. The music was low again and so was she, staring out the window, arms folded across her chest. She was probably going to leave it and maybe that would be for the best. Let it break apart amid one of the rare moments—watching her go from a thousand miles away from him to charming the gruff off a Mexican border guard, then back to a thousand miles away—where he didn't trust her heart and knew that he never should have. Not for one day.

Emmavail picked up Webster, sat Indian style in her seat and closed her eyes. "Why does my boyfriend think that I want to be with a man who knows what it's like to be set on fire, when what I really want, what I've always wanted, is a man who would do anything to protect me from that?" she said, flipping through the pages.

"I don't want to play."

"How about this one then? Why does my boyfriend have a dog hidden in his trunk?"

Fuck it, he thought.

Brandon pulled over, got out, and popped the trunk. The dog was thrilled to see him, to be alive, to be in a trunk. He was thrilled when Brandon told him to go ahead and hop down. The dog sat down in the backseat and Brandon got them moving again.

"You never said stop," Emmavail said. The dictionary sat flat on her lap like a thing that once contained air. "You just left me here flipping pages."

"I don't need Webster to tell me what I already know."

"Brando. You don't know shit."

The needle at eighty, Brandon thought about all of the millions of cars in the world filled with the millions of people who were not having this conversation. All of the boyfriends who weren't trying to break up with their girlfriends they didn't really want to break up with before they got the chance to do it first. He envied all of them.

"He smells like hot vomit," said Emmavail. "He is a he, isn't he?"

"He is." Brandon rolled down his window, but the air whipping at the ragged fur only released new smells.

"You're going to name him Argonaut," she said. "Aren't you?"

"I was thinking about it."

Emmavail closed her eyes and pressed Webster to her forehead. "Why does my boyfriend not understand that getting married and having babies and liberating dogs from foreign countries are things he's supposed to do with his girlfriend?"

She flipped through the pages, and Brandon said, "Stop."

"Oblivious. The inability to see what's right in your face."

"Freaky."

"That was me talking," she said. "Webster said pantaloons but that doesn't make any fucking sense."

Brandon took his sunglasses off Emmavail's face, put them on himself, and said, "Do you want to do those things?"

"Get married?"

"Yeah."

"Have babies?"

"Yeah."

"Liberate dogs from foreign countries?"

"All those things," he said.

She took back the sunglasses like he knew she would, put them back on, twisted around in her seat, and scratched Argonaut behind his ears.

"Well," she said. "We've already got the dog."

I USED TO KNOW THIS PLACE

BONES AND SIDNEY LOVED EACH OTHER LIKE SOLDIERS AND PITIED ALL friendships not their own. In their last winter of high school, they rattled down Main Street in Bones' '82 Civic. The yet-to-be-overturned zoning laws of Hunnsicker Township prohibited change, one side of Main Street a city green and gazebo, the other a train of antique stores, candle stores, and an old-fashioned soda fountain called Saywell's. Behind Main Street sprawled vast nothing, back roads and barren, loping fields of snow and mud.

They turned onto those back roads, off Main, no destination in mind, Sidney saying he'd lost all interest in living in the wake of a breakup with a girl named Annie, Bones not believing him.

"I don't believe you," said Bones.

"Am I lying?"

"I don't think you're lying. I just don't believe you."

Miles of fresh chain-link fence and SOLD signs jigsawed the earth, random metal chomps taken out of what had always been open and endless and theirs.

"Where did these fences come from?" said Bones.

"I don't even know how I would begin caring about that," said Sidney.

"Your ire lacks authority. You woke up this morning and showered and brushed your hair and put on clean clothes. These are not the actions of a soon-to-be dead man."

"What do I have to do to prove it?"

"Die," said Bones.

"All right," said Sidney. "Kill me."

The alignment of Bones' '82 Civic was off. If he did not keep the wheel crooked to the left, the car veered towards the berm. If it had its way, the car would list only in lazy circles the size of a lake. Bones took his hands off the wheel and laced his fingers behind his head.

"All right," said Bones.

"All right, what?"

"I'm not gonna right this car. You are. Because you want to live."

Sidney crossed his arms tight across his chest. "Bet me," he said.

"I already have," said Bones.

Picking up speed, they passed the old hangar some artist used for her studio. It sat still and strange in the snow, a half-buried HoHo painted bar-soap green. Like the rest of the familiar nothing, it too was caged in silver fence and SOLD signs.

"Annie was it," said Sidney. "There are no other Annies."

"Annie's half as funny as she needs to be." Bones took off his seat belt. "All she really has going for her is that everyone loves her."

"You only think you know what you know," said Sidney, undoing his seat belt. "The end result of your wrongness is going to be ghastly."

"When we don't die," Bones said, "man are you gonna look like an idiot."

"When we do die," said Sidney, "man are you gonna look dead."

With every bump, the wheel flinched like a polygraph needle. The road's vanishing point dragged driver's side in the windshield, Bones and Sidney adjusting their posture to the pull of this new gravity. Easing into its freedom, the Civic was going to break apart or fly. It hadn't decided yet.

"She used to ask me how my parents raised me," said Sidney. "She said that's how she was going to raise her kids."

"That's one of those things that's so easy to say if you can think of it," said Bones.

The passenger side wheels were off pavement, kicking up slushy gravel.

"You're going to right this wheel."

"And I think you're going to be very surprised by what happens next."

Up ahead, the road narrowed underneath an abandoned railroad bridge. The little tunnel was haunted, everyone said. When you passed through with the windows down, you could hear the moans of some prom queen ghost bouncing off the walls. The Civic settled on the right support wall as its destination.

"My heart is a collapsing star."

"I won't let them put that on your headstone."

Half off the road, ice-capped branches clicked against Sidney's window. Brown icicles hung from the rusted-out bridge. The approaching wall, stone blocks the size of ottomans, grew larger and larger until they could see the moss calking the cracks. Fifty-seven miles an hour and getting faster.

"Wake me when all this is over," said Bones, reclining his seat back, draping the inside of his elbow over his eyes.

Sidney turned around, sat Indian style, and leaned his back against the dashboard. "Me," he said, "I'm just working on my tan."

Bones would return to Hunnsicker years later to find that those back roads, those barren fields he once knew like he now knows the difference between good whiskey and bad, were gone. Gone. Replaced by the new Hunnsicker. Boutiques, salons, dress stores, jewelry stores, cell phone stores, ice creameries where kids pounded M&Ms and gummi bears into the ice cream right before your eyes. These stores for miles.

And for miles Bones walked the unrecognizable ground. Limped actually, if anyone was paying attention, up and down clean sidewalk and storefronts so new they looked wet. If he could find where the artist's hangar used to be, he told himself, he'd be only a half-mile east of where it happened, where he came to—right ankle turned into paste, left tibia and femur jutting out through muscle and skin—and saw sheet-metal sky through a Sidney-sized hole in his windshield.

When he thought he had found it, standing in front of a store that sold copper pots and pans, his first impulse was to find Sidney and ask him who it was in Hunnsicker that needed copper pots and pans.

"An all-grown-up Annie," Sidney would have said. "A show wife puttering around her show kitchen. That's who."

"Oh, yeah," Bones would say. "Her."

"Yep. Her."

"Yet you'll still tell me it was worth it? Launching yourself through a windshield, cracking your skull and spine and smearing your insides twenty feet down a salty strip of black road? All because of some girl destined to be an average wife for average men?"

"Absolutely worth it. One-hundred percent. Because that is what love means to me."

"I don't believe you," Bones would say.

"Am I lying?"

"I don't think you're lying. I just don't believe you."

And for a moment there had never been a day where everything changed. For a moment, in Bones' mind, he and Sidney are two grown men who drink Jeppson's Malört while talking on the phone once a week. About how Bones had talked Sidney out of three bad marriages or how Sidney had talked Bones into one good one, to the woman who didn't get away, who maybe really did love him for real. Or how they'll never return to Hunnsicker to see what's become of the old place or to imagine who they might have become if things had been just a little different. Like that day we almost smashed into the railroad bridge before you righted the wheel.

Depressing, they'd agree. Enough of that. Now let us kill these bottles so that we might get back to the lives we are so thankful to be living.

But only for a moment.

THE GLITTER AND THE ROAR

SHE WAS OLIVE THOMAS. FAMOUS SHOWGIRL AND SILENT FILM STAR and winner of the 1914 *Most Beautiful Girl in New York City* contest and twenty-five years old and if she wanted cocaine she would have it. But all night, all over Montmartre, she had not found enough. A few bumps at Fontaine de la Jeunesse. A few at the illusionist's apartment. No more. And there was none, she knew, in her and Jack's suite at The Ritz.

Her husband, Jack Pickford, younger brother of Mary Pickford—*the* Mary Pickford—lay splayed across a maroon divan, his suit jacket underneath his head, his red cravat undone about his neck like a slit throat. Olive—Ollie to her friends; she had lots of friends—dropped the room key to the floor, kicked off her shoes with two thumps, and dragged her black silk gown over her head and off her torso. She walked in black rayon stockings, garter belt, and step-in panties to the bar. With a tiny hand she held a tumbler and with another she filled it with brown liquor.

"If I tried to fuck you tonight," Jack said without opening his eyes, "I can't guarantee you I'd finish."

"Don't put yourself out, fella," she said, gliding, heavy-lidded, through the dark, candle-licked air and into the bathroom.

She set the tumbler on the marble countertop. One candle in a brass candlestick made the shadows of perfume bottles and brushes and jewelry long and shaky. The girl in the mirror existed from the waist up and only faintly. An alabaster shadow of soft curves.

"The Most Beautiful Girl in the World," she said to no one.

Jack's leather toiletry bag was filed with blue and brown bottles. Olive took one into her hand and tried to read the label. It was in French. Close enough. She opened the bottle and dropped a fistful of tablets into the tumbler, several scattering across the marble, into the sink, onto the floor. After a night of champagne cocktails and everything raucous and fucking dogs, she would have sleep if she could not have cocaine. She drank.

The sharp flame of the candle became a dandelion puff. She thought of the hotel bed and how she must hurry. As she turned, her knees buckled and she dropped to the cold black and white tiles. She picked up one of the tablets. Color of bone. The shape of a coffin. Mercury Bichloride, she knew then. Jack's syphilis treatment. For external use only. Her limbs tingled. A gluey mass burning in her stomach, she clawed herself off the ground with dead hands and staggered out of the bathroom door, upright and rickety, on dead feet.

"My God," she said through dead lips, "what have I done?"

It was three twenty-seven am. She was dying. She was already dead.

Outside the nameless bar, Olive and Percy, arm-in-arm, swaying to nonexistent music in a Big Bertha crater, she wanted him to keep talking. About walking to a train station that very night. Hopping a freight car north. Stowing away aboard a steamer. Stealing blankets and hiding inside a lifeboat on their backs for days, staring at the stars through a tear in the canvas top.

"I've done a lot of things in holes like this," said Percy. "Eaten, shaved, slept. Seen men blown to pieces. Never fallen in love."

Olive couldn't count the number of times she'd fallen in love. Couldn't count the number or recall the places. Name the city. The bar. The party.

There was always some man or two. She'd fallen in and out of love with Jack at least five times every day she'd known him.

Over Percy's shoulder, The Ritz towered in its orange hue above the blackened and jagged canyon of two-story storefronts. She swore she could see their suite, her and Jack's. Could see Jack himself staring out the window and into the light-dotted cityscape for his beautiful little girl.

"I recommend falling in love anywhere you can," she said.

"I don't doubt that you do."

She pressed her chest to his, her face to his neck. "Tell me more," she said.

"Or we could just go. We could go right now."

"No. Not just yet," she said. "Tell me what the rest of my life would be like."

"'Would'?" he said. "Or 'will'?"

"Either."

His dancing slowed. His hold on her body slackened. "It won't be like you think."

"You lie," she laughed.

He let her go, peeled her off his front and hopped out of the chasm. "Maybe we should just call it a night."

"But why would we do that?" she said, climbing out of the hole, clattering after him in her heels. "There's so much night left."

"Because you're ending up there," he said, pointing at The Ritz with his thumb. "And I'm not. And I'm tired."

"You know everything all of a sudden?"

Percy buttoned his tuxedo jacket and turned up the collar about his neck as if realizing just then the air was cold. He scanned the empty block, then looked up at The Ritz.

"I'd get on my knees and beg you to go with me if I thought you would."

Making people believe her face was her job. The only job she was ever good at. Tonight, right now, Percy was her camera lens. Look torn and hurt, she told herself. Wear a thousand feelings on your face all at once. When the words won't come, tears will instead, and he will see that she is worth trading in his whole life for just a piece of hers.

"Fine," he said, shaking his head. "You're miserable. The life you lead is rotten. The man you married is an ass. Come with me."

Her chin stopped trembling. Her eyes went dry. She looked at his upturned collar, his white breath, his shot, sleepless eyes, and knew he was right. It *was* cold. And late. She had to be getting back.

"So handsome," she said, and stroked his face.

Walking in the direction of The Ritz, down the sidewalk, in and out of the wavy gas lamp shadows, she knew he would watch her until she disappeared around a corner. There were a thousand Percys, ten in every bright and jumping room, at least. The ones who couldn't give her things always wanted to save her from something. And maybe, she thought, one day, when all of this gets to be too much, she might let one of them do just that.

But not tonight. Because he doesn't love her. Not really. He couldn't. That would be ridiculous. And if she didn't love Jack, and if the love of all those people out there wasn't what she always wanted, wasn't enough, then what was all of this worth?

"Not a goddamn thing," she said to the gray bricks, the cobblestones like river rocks, the wood crates spilling with cabbage leaves and potato peels. "Not a goddamn thing."

Olive stopped the cab and paid the man with a fistful of funny-colored money and said, "Keep it." She and Percy stepped out onto a bleak stretch of cobblestoned street pocked with artillery craters. The Ritz, not three blocks off, loomed and glowed above a procession of bombed-out two-stories.

I heard there's a bar here that's crazy," said Olive. "No name or sign. Just a picture of an elephant on the door."

"A place like that sounds like trouble," said Percy, smiling coolly, as though his definition of trouble was a thing inconvenient and silly.

"Trouble." Olive's eyes popped wild. She clutched onto Percy's arm, knocking him back. "That's what I want. Let's find some trouble we can't buy our way out of."

"I have the feeling that won't be hard."

By the flicker of streetlamps, they found a brass placard in the shape of an elephant. They pushed through the heavy wooden door and into a room the size of a train car. Warm reds and deep browns and patinaed gas lamps that absorbed more light than they produced. A man with a head turbaned with grimed bandages lay slumped over the bar, his hand wrapped around an empty glass. Another man in a once-white apron stood behind the bar counting something Olive could not see.

"Not exactly crazy," said Percy.

They sat at one of the four tables and drank what might have been turpentine. Their cigarette smoke clouded the air, her hands stuck to the table, and she examined spots on the floor that might be blood. Unclean. Unsafe. And Percy was not Jack.

"I love it."

The Great Hyperion had told her about this place, regaled her with stories of gangsters and knife fights and human life for sale in the back rooms. She said it sounded like Paramount.

"That fella," she whispered. "With the turban. Is he a swami?"

"He has a hole in his skull," he said, running a hand through her thin, black bob. "He wears that to protect his brain."

"How bizarre. Was he a soldier?"

Percy nodded yes. "Or a very unlucky bystander."

"You were a soldier," said Olive.

"I was."

She imagined Percy in uniform, mud spattered, rifle slung over his shoulder, shrugging off buzzing bullets and explosions rumbling the ground with the same detachment as he did a room full of rich cunts and big-talking men.

"How did that happen?"

"I had nowhere to go and nothing to do when I got there." He shrugged. "It seemed as good an idea as any other."

"You're the kind of man who does things."

"Am I?"

"I heard you talking to those women at the restaurant. Stowing away. Riding the rails." Olive straightened her back, lowered her chin, and did a nasal mimic of the women from Fontaine de la Jeunesse. "*Oh, Mr. Percy. You brute. Do go on. Do go on.*"

"If I told you about all that," Percy said, "what would make you any different from them?"

The man in the apron came out from behind the bar and tapped the turbaned man between the shoulder blades. He stirred, tried several times to lift himself before thudding back onto the bar. The bartender persisted, tapping him again, hoisting the drunk's arm across his own neck and walking him to the door, the drunk moving like a sack of sawdust.

"I think we're next," said Percy.

"Because I would go with you."

"What was that?"

"That's what makes me different," Olive said. "Because I would go with you."

She stepped out of The Great Hyperion's building, underneath a blood orange awning, the cool air drying the perspiration sheening her body. She felt fresh and burgeoning, like a newborn. Percy was there, too, sitting next to a fern and smoking a cigarette.

"You," she said, and smiled.

"Me," he said.

"You're the only thing tonight that has made me happy." She looked down at her own shoes.

"If I had a watch I would tell you the night is young." He stood and walked to her. "But I don't have a watch, and I'd be lying anyways."

He reached the cigarette out to her and she took it. She inhaled and let the smoke drift out of the side of her mouth.

"What are you going to do when you run out of money?"

"I haven't thought about it," he said, taking back the cigarette. "Die, I suppose."

Her arms at her waist, she pressed her head to his chest. He smelled of smoke and linen. "Don't die."

He threw the cigarette into the street and held her bare arms. "You're so small."

"You can kiss me hard if you want." Her chin just below his bowtie. "I've sweat away most of my makeup, I think. You won't smear anything."

He kissed her gently, their lips touching for less than a second. She closed her eyes and waited for more. When she opened them again, he was leaning back, studying her face. He was sad.

A black taxicab sidled up next to them. He held onto her for a few moments, then let her go. She bowed her head and stared hard at an ivory button on his shirt.

"Come in here with me," she said, tugging his sleeve. "We're going somewhere."

"I haven't turned down a single invitation tonight. What brand of man would I be if I turned down this one?"

"An idiot," Olive said, tumbling headfirst into the back of the cab. She allowed her backside to hover in the air a few moments before settling into seat, disappointed Percy had not slid his hand across its silk. He entered the cab and clunked the door closed behind him. The driver pressed the accelerator. Clean lights snaked across the hood and windows of the taxi as she curled herself into Percy, realizing for the first time that there were so many men she would never get to marry.

The air in The Great Hyperion's apartment was hot and getting hotter with bodies and action. Olive walked across the parquet dance floor, through the flailing arms and upturned feet and swinging pearls. That song from last year wound to a finish and some voices shouted "Again!" and others "Encore!" The Great Hyperion, his silk shirt untucked and plastered with sweat to his oval torso, shuffled and snapped a deck of cards and asked the Belgian heiress and one of the men wearing a beret to "Pick a card. Any old card."

"Be a dear," Olive said, the same song swelling to life again on the Victrola. "Fetch me a cab."

"Darling!" The Great Hyperion shouted. "Darling. Let me get you not a cab but another drink."

"I'm all drunk out, I think."

"Did you find any—?" said the Great Hyperion, tapping his right nostril.

She shook her head no and looked at the Belgian heiress, knowing in her hand was a gold compact full of white powder.

"What sort of host am I?" he said, shaking his head. "What sort of host am I?"

"I know your face," said the bereted man. "Vargas painted you."

"If you've seen that painting," said Olive, clutching her breasts through the shapeless silk of her dress, "then you know these, too."

The Great Hyperion bellowed.

"Everyone at this party has been well-acquainted with those, my dear," said the heiress.

"Vargas is a whore," said the man in the beret.

"Coming from a Frog and his cash cow, that's a compliment," said The Great Hyperion. He set a heavy arm around Olive's shoulders and led her away from his tiny, indifferent audience. "Don't mind the trash."

"He's a fag and she looks like her mother fucked a horse."

The Great Hyperion bellowed again and said, "I can attest on both counts. And neither one believes in magic."

"Fetch me a cab."

"I will," he said, shooting the deck of cards from hand to the other. "My Darling, if there were a Queen of Saucy Cunts, I'd pull it from behind your ear."

*

The Great Hyperion, more famous for his soirees than his act anymore, buzzed from guest to guest, refilling drinks and calling everyone "Darling." The collie with the black top hat tied under his chin and bowtie around his neck like a collar humped away on the bored-looking poodle with the wedding veil tied to her head. This was happening ten inches from Olive's foot.

"Tell me about it, sister," Olive said to the poodle. "I hope he bought you a steak dinner first."

At the same time she wished Jack was still there and that she had never met him. Olive was lonely and the fucking dogs made her want to do something unabashed and animal. When she got back to the suite, she knew Jack would be unconscious or mostly unconscious and up for nothing. She wished she hadn't said what she'd said to him. She wished it wasn't true.

"It makes you think," said the man in the shabby tuxedo. He approached from behind, resting his elbows on the chair next to Olive.

"Whatta 'bout?" she said, aware she was slurring a little.

"All of the unfortunate puppies born out of wedlock."

Across the room, Rudolph Valentino sat doing shots with two showgirls from Fontaine de la Jeunesse, one in her beaded, emerald-green dress and cap stage costume, the other in an angular suit cut for a man. Olive looked into her own half-full glass, didn't want it, and knew there was nothing more alcohol could do for her tonight.

"Your name is Percy," said Olive, patting the chair next to her, beckoning him to sit.

"And you're Olive. You seem to be a pretty big to-do."

"Oh, but I am. Couldn't you tell? Sitting here all alone," she said. "And what are you doing here, Percy?"

"This party or Paris?"

"Both."

"This party," he said, sitting next to her, not looking away from the dogs, "because I was getting drunk at Fontaine de la Jeunesse and The Great

Hyperion mistook me for important. Paris because it's as good as any other place to spend what's left of your money."

Someone played a song from last year on the Victrola. Several bodies left the parquet dance floor and more than several entered.

"You seem to have a knack tonight," said Olive, "for getting me to notice you."

"It's harder than it looks."

"It doesn't look that hard."

"It isn't," he said. "And you? What are you doing here?"

"My honeymoon."

"That's funny. That's just what this poodle told me."

Someone turned up the Victrola. Valentino was now drinking alone. The collie began to yowl.

"It won't last though," he went on.

"Why not?" She thought again of Jack. "Because it never does?"

He pointed to the poodle. "Because she's a bitch."

Olive put her drink down and took hold of Percy by his lapels. She pressed her cheek to his and closed her eyes.

"You're adorable and poor," she whispered. "I should lick your face so you never forget tonight."

"That's funny. That's just what this poodle told me."

Since her arrival at The Great Hyperion's party, Olive switched from champagne cocktails to the whiskeys people put into her hands. She was on her fourth, dancing wild on the parquet floor. Jack on his first sat slouched in a chair muttering, "I'm okay. I'm okay," to no one. His skin was pallid and damp and his recent inability to maintain himself into their busy nights annoyed her. She walked to him.

"I'm okay," he said. "I'm okay."

"No. You're not."

Jack set down his whiskey and grated his hands up and down his face and hair. "No," he said. "I don't suppose I am."

Olive put her hands on her hips. All of the other men at the party were vibrant, impressive, red of cheek. Different versions of the Jack Pickford who'd wooed Olive up and down Hollywood.

"Some honeymoon."

"These nights," he looked up at her, "just get so long."

"Dunk your head in some cold water," she said, shaking him by the shoulder.

"Sweetheart, I think I'm gonna head back to the hotel."

He hoisted himself up and made an awkward gesture towards Olive, as though he wasn't sure whether he would hug her or kiss her. She put a hand to his mouth and brushed him away, allowing him neither.

The man, Percy, sat alone on a footstool before a blazing fireplace balancing a silver tray candled with champagne flutes. One by one, he opened his throat and downed each flute before shattering it into the fireplace.

That's what a man who's alive looks like, Olive thought.

She turned back towards Jack, towards his slouched-shouldered stagger away from her and to the exit. When the nights lose their momentum, when opened doors leading to drinks and more drinks will take them no further, this is what Olive is left with. In none of it can she find a forever that appeals to her.

"Yeah," she yelled. "Take your rotted cock and get outta here!"

She wanted him to react, to shout terrible and true things from across the room. To prove something masculine and mean with his fists. To make a scene. Some people close by stopped what they were doing and watched. Most in the room though did not and the music went on uninterrupted.

"Ya hear me?"

His movement away from her was slow and defeated. Bodies bumped into him. The faces didn't notice much and neither did Jack. He walked out the door.

Olive poured his whiskey into her glass and looked around. The bystanders were sinking back into conversations of thirty seconds ago. Beyond them, the Belgian heiress from Fontaine de la Juenesse sat on a brown leather sectional.

Her entourage reached into her gold makeup compact and did bumps from off their pinky fingers.

When Olive got to the sectional, the five or six of them were speaking a language Olive did not know. The compact was closed.

"I'm sorry," said Olive, tapping her nose. "But you wouldn't happen to have some—?"

"I'm so sorry, my dear," said the heiress, setting her hand on the compact as though it might float away. "I was just about to ask you that same question."

Half of the patrons from Fontaine de la Jeunesse, and a few random people picked up along the three-block walk through Montmartre, filed into The Great Hyperion's apartment. Facing a trellis of roses sat two clusters of chairs, a small aisle separating them down the center. A priest sat in one of the chairs leafing through a Bible. With great arm gestures and his booming voice, The Great Hyperion ushered his guests into the chairs and the priest to his side underneath the trellis.

Jack stretched out to her right, bored and drunk. To her left, the man in the shabby tuxedo—Percy—sat swirling the ice in a glass he'd lifted from Fontaine de la Jeunesse.

"Ladies and Gentlemen!" The Great Hyperion raised his arms high into the air. "The moment you have been waiting for but did not know you were waiting for has arrived."

He snapped his fingers. "Ode to Joy" played from somewhere and a collie wearing a top hat and a poodle wearing a veil walked side-by-side down the aisle. The laughter changed from titters to uproar. The Great Hyperion held up one hand. "Please, Ladies and Gentleman. This moment calls for solemnity."

The music cut off. The dogs sat before the priest as he performed the ceremony. If he thought there was anything at all unusual to any of this, the priest gave no indication. When the poodle was to say "I do," The Great Hyperion snapped his fingers and she barked. With the collie's turn, he snapped them again. The collie barked and the attendants exploded with cheer.

"No one in this room has, in their lives, raised a revolver to their temple with any real conviction, and I have to believe much of that can be attributed to love," said The Great Hyperion. "Love in all of its vaguatries. Remember what you've seen here tonight."

"I don't think 'vaguatries' is a word," Percy whispered to Olive. "But I'm moved none the less."

Olive too was moved. She wiped a tear from her face with a kerchief, stuffed it back into her tiny purse, and waited for Jack to take her hand. Or to whisper something sweet and private into her ear. To acknowledge that they were in on this thing together; their life as man and wife. That he forgave her for all of the other men and then she would forgive him for all of the women, for injecting her with disease, for everything. And then they would dance.

The Great Hyperion clapped his hands and the collie, as he was trained, mounted the poodle and began fucking her. The crowd laughed and shouted and whistled. Dance music swelled. Jack checked his watch and lit a cigarette.

Fontaine de la Juenesse was bright and busy and Olive and Jack's table was at its epicenter. White-jacketed waiters cleared dinner plates and set down two pink desserts before them. Jack's hand crept from the small of her back to the soft curve of her buttock as he ordered another round. A stage full of leggy French girls jingling with emerald beads kicked the air and slapped each other's bottoms with wild grins to the brassy mayhem of a band half-made up of Negroes. Olive was finishing her fifth champagne cocktail and it and the four previous were really thrumming.

"What did we just eat?" she asked.

"A lot," said Jack.

"I love this feeling," she said, closing her eyes and leaning back into her chair.

"What feeling is that, sweetheart?"

"That the whole world was made for us."

"Who's saying it wasn't?" said Jack, leaning over and kissing Olive on the neck.

The Great Hyperion emerged into the bistro through a swinging kitchen door and Olive clapped her hands with glee. She'd met him in 1915 while working Ziegfeld's Midnight Frolics at the New Amsterdam Theatre in New York. After the show one night, the two of them drinking gin and Olive wearing what was left of an outfit made only of balloons, The Great Hyperion told her, "On the days I'm not queer, you're all I think about."

"All of these beautiful people!" The Great Hyperion shouted, wearing a white suit and a maroon fez on his bald head. "Shoveling food and drink into their mouths!"

The men and women of the room, the band, and the showgirls cheered, then hushed with anticipation.

"Do my eyes deceive me or is the most beautiful one of all amongst you?" He shaded his eyes with his hand. "Why, is that young Ms. Ollie Thomas?"

Olive stood atop two chairs and held out her arms to applause.

"The Flapper. The Baby Vamp," said The Great Hyperion. "The Most Beautiful Girl in New York."

"Tonight," said Jack, "the Most Beautiful Girl in Paris."

"Hell," said Olive, putting her hands to her hips. "The World!"

The Great Hyperion quelled the din of applause and looked about the room. He put two fingers to his temple and closed his eyes.

"I am having a vision, Young Miss Ollie. What all of this fine living has in store for you." He pulled up his shirt, revealing a pale, bloated belly. He slapped it twice. "Gaze into my crystal ball and see your future."

"That's tomorrow! This is tonight!" Olive shouted and pulled down the front of her dress, flashing her breasts to a serenade of catcalls and whistles and a trumpeter playing some grungy, lowdown notes.

"And who's that with you if not Mary Pickford's little brother?" he said. "Before I met Little Jackie, I thought nepotism was a breathing disorder."

Even those who pretended not to speak English roared with laughter.

"Why don't you make yourself disappear," said Jack.

"I intend to. In fact, let all of us disappear. Darlings. Dearhearts. Men of men. You are all invited to make this public party private."

Following The Great Hyperion, much of the crowd flowed towards the exit. Olive looked down at Jack, at the vacant grin of a fool who did not know he was a fool. She was more famous than he. More beautiful. More loved. And he was with her.

"Catch me, you goon," she said.

Jack set some money on the table. Olive tilted off the chairs and landed in Jack's arms. He carried her within the current of fine women smoking long, dark cigarettes escorted by handsome, glowing men, and they were the only two not giggling like children.

The doors of Fontaine de la Jeunesse were opened for them and the maitre d' recognized Olive and Jack immediately. He raced to them and took Olive's hands into his. "*Mes petits enfants,*" he cooed. Then, in English, "Don't worry. Don't worry." He slipped away, whispered something to a busboy, and disappeared into the ballroom.

The waiting lounge was blue with cigarette smoke and crowded with men and women unaccustomed to waits. A tall woman with a prominent chin and brow stood rigid before the maitre d' desk. Her party consisted of glum-looking men wearing berets.

"Who's that?" asked Olive.

"Some Belgian heiress. I met her once. I really should remember her name."

"She looks serious."

"She is."

"Introduce me," said Olive, her mouth curling into a smile.

"I just told you," said Jack. "I don't remember her name."

"Introduce me."

Jack shrugged, put his hand on the small of Olive's back, and walked her the two feet separating them from the Belgian heiress. She recognized Jack, smiled faintly, and they kissed cheeks.

"So good to see you again," said Jack.

"Indeed."

"Have you met my wife?"

"The movie star," said the heiress. Her tone was somewhere between a statement and a question.

The women took each other's hands, palms down, in a delicate gesture of pure understanding. That the heiress was richer and Olive was prettier. That the heiress, underneath her hereditary politeness, thought Olive was a whore. Olive, for her part, was well aware the heiress was the wife or sister or mother of the men who lavished her with pearls and diamonds and minks since her late teens.

"Indeed," said Olive, releasing her hand.

Olive paid no mind to the awkward silence that followed, to Jack's nodding at nothing, to the heiress and her artist-types pursing their lips, waiting to continue their conversation interrupted by this "movie star" and her husband. Another party off to her right, or the bits and pieces of several parties, held her attention. A group of women, old-money Brits, Olive guessed, away from their husbands and searching for wild stories of their own, each jeweled and gowned in lime greens and pinks like shimmering, lumpy sherbet. They flocked and chattered around a tall American. He wore a tuxedo that had seen better days, his white shirt yellowing at the collar and frayed at the cuffs.

"Mr. Percy," one of the women said, "was just telling us about the time he jumped from a moving train while running from a man with a loaded pistol."

With sharp, high-angled eyebrows that gave him the air of a wood sprite, Olive found him quite striking. As did the Brits, laughing at his every word, covering their toothy smiles with gloved hands like geishas.

"I can't guarantee you it was loaded," said the man.

"Oh, yes," said another woman, as though she and this man were old, old friends. "Mr. Percy has been absolutely everywhere and, if we are to believe him, he's not once paid for passage."

"If I don't know where I'm going," he said, crushing out his cigarette into a glass ash stand at his knee, "why should I pay for it?"

The women fumbled through their purses, five gold cigarette cases snapping open before him. He chose one, followed by more fumbling and the sparking of five gold cigarette lighters.

"Cheers," he said.

"But wouldn't simply buying the ticket be so much easier?"

"I plan ahead in my own way. So long as you ladies are passing out cigarettes buffet style, it's only fair that I have stories to tell."

"A man like you, Mr. Percy," said the woman he took the cigarette from, "I thought would 'roll his own', as they say."

"That is what we say. In fact, it's in the scoundrel's handbook."

Olive laughed at this, as if only she and this man could appreciate the absurdity of these women, their gripping so tight to a life and youth they never knew. "Did you hear that?" she asked, tugging on Jack's arm.

"I'm gonna be honest with you, Ollie," said Jack, looking dumbly about the room. "I'm not just a little peckish."

She ignored that, its disconnect from anything she found even remotely interesting right then, and returned to making the Belgian heiress uncomfortable.

"Have you all been waiting long?"

"Not long," the heiress said. "A minor problem, I'm sure."

"I'm sure."

"Mr. Percy," Olive heard. "Do dine with us."

"I'm sorry, ladies. If you need me, I'll be having a whiskey sandwich at the bar."

The maitre d' glided back into the lounge. "*Madam. Monsieur*," he said to Olive and Jack. "This way." He led them from the small room to the large as though the universe itself were expanding just for them. For her.

She looked back at the man in the shabby tuxedo. Through all the smoke, his exhaling, the women exhaling towards him, he met her glance, cocked one of his fairytale eyebrows, and bowed his head to her. She winked to him over her shoulder, then winked at the Belgian heiress for good measure.

*

The sun was setting and the low light made the rooms of the suite glow dark gold. Olive was sitting on a maroon divan when Jack finally emerged from the steaming bathroom. He was, as usual, cleaner than she, powdered and slick, wearing a red silk cravat under a palmetto collar and the dark suit he'd bought in London.

"How do I look?" he said.

"Like a dandy," she said, flicking her wrist.

His grooming ritual included applying his Mercury Bichloride solution and taking something from one the bottles in his leather toiletry bag to bring him up or take him down. He was up, she could tell, for now. Olive patted the space next to her on the divan and Jack sat with her.

He didn't look sick. He didn't look like a liar. And Olive herself did not feel like a chump or a liar for not wondering what cunt made him sick, how many cunts he'd passed it on to, was still passing it on to, that she herself probably had it, that one day all of this would come to an end and what would she do then?

She looked at the rings on her left hand. The pearl ring on her middle finger. A gift from an admirer. An oil baron. He gave it to her the first month she worked the Follies for Ziegfeld. On the next finger, her wedding band. She wore them always and looked at them when she needed to be reminded what it was to be poor and unloved.

"How do I look?" she said.

"Happy," he said.

Olive coiled her arms around Jack's arm, buried her face into his shoulder, and put it out of her mind that she did not believe him.

SUCH BEAUTIFUL PLACES

Akron, OH, 1919

When it was obvious her husband would not be coming home that night at a decent hour, or at all, from walking his beat or drinking with the boys, Emma Baron went to church. Only her oldest child knew what she meant by "church." The neighborhood movie house, which had been St. Paul's Methodist until the Christmas tree money was absconded with over the minister's beaten-to-death body the previous December. Both parents gone and spending money the family could not spare, Henry, a dutiful and serious fifteen, was left to care for his four younger sisters.

"Is Mama bringing food?" one of the girls would ask.

"Of course she is. What do you hope she brings you?"

Eula wanted oranges. Mixie wanted sausages. Mary and Georgia wanted candy, the kind with stripes, which they'd only had once in their lives. Henry kept them talking, all tucked into a single bed, until the girls drifted off to sleep and wouldn't have to see their mother's empty arms.

The Baron home was a two-room shack overlooking the valley on the outskirts of downtown Akron, Ohio. The girls huddled in their bed, Henry sat at the table, stoked the stove embers, and knew better than to sleep. The moment his mother returned from "church," his lessons began.

He never knew what time to expect her. Late. That was all. Waiting, no
way to mark the time, he sometimes imagined her walk from the defunct
church, step-for-step. A woman alone, street lamps spilling her shaky shadow
over the brick-laid streets, making her way past Miller's Lumber Yard, the
butcher's cattle pen, dangerously oblivious to everything around her.

When she finally made it home, Emma Baron glided through the door
like some noblewoman, exaggerating all her movements. She slowly peeled
off her cloche hat and overcoat and spectered across the tiny room as though
newspaper-insulated planks were vaulted ceilings and marble. As though
Henry were a thousand courtesans. Smiling dreamily, eyes almost closed, she
sat down next to him, lit a candle, and placed a ruler flat onto the table.

"Was it a good show, Mother?"

He had never seen a movie. All he had to draw from was what his mother
described each night. Castles and manors in faraway places. Dashing men
fighting scoundrels with pistols and sabers, the virtue and sometimes the life
of some gowned, jeweled girl hanging in the balance. And each night, she
described these faraway places as though that's where she'd been this whole
time and those gowned, jeweled girls were her.

"Oh. Oh, Henry." Her smile grew wide. "There are such wonderful places
in this world. And you will see them all."

"Yes, Mother."

"That is if you don't turn out ignorant gutter trash like your sisters and
father."

"Yes, Mother."

"Are you ready?" his mother asked, picking up the ruler. He had no choice
but to be ready. "Say, 'I can't go on.'"

"'I can't go on,'" he repeated, and his mother struck him across the cheek
with the ruler.

"How did you sound just now?"

"Gutter trash."

"Yes. Gutter trash. Now say it right."

"'I *cahnt* go on,'" said Henry.

"Yes, my darling boy. Say it again."

"I *cahnt* go on."

"Beautiful." She clapped her hands, still clutching the ruler. "Now say, 'Such a wonderful evening.'"

"'Such a *wund-a-full* evening.'"

And the lesson went on, for hours sometimes, Emma Baron preparing Henry to take his rightful place in her dream world. A world she paid a dime to inhabit, that infected her mind for days—asking the grocer for "*anoth-ah cahn* of peas" with a pursed, girlish grin. A world that must have seemed like such a tragic joke when she found herself back in her real life.

She appeared to be at her most lucid when both parents were home, fighting like jackals. Henry found a strange comfort in those fights, taking his sisters outside if it was daytime. Holding Eula, Mixie, Georgia and Mary close while yells and pounding rattled their parents' door at night. It meant they weren't alone. It meant, Henry thought, that he was not all that stood between his sisters and death.

During these fights, Emma Baron relished every opportunity to describe to her husband what her life would have been like if not for him. If not for his drinking, his nothing salary, his dirt blood. And it could all be traced back to this boy she knew from school. He was from England, she'd say, and everything he said sounded like a poem.

"He was beautiful, like I was. Everything he did was beautiful and everything you do is dirt."

"Then go find him," John Baron would say. "Go not cook for him. Go not raise his kids. If you can even remember his name. If he ever knew yours."

"'*For-evah*,'" repeated Henry, cold, grey morning light edging through the cracks in the walls, dully glowing the butcher paper greased to the windows.

"'I will be with you forever.'"

"'I will be with you *for-evah*.'"

"Yes, yes. You did *wund-a-full*, Henry Baron," she said. "My beautiful boy. Are you listening?"

"Yes, Mother."

"This house. This town. All the towns everywhere just like this one and worse. Do you know what they are?" Henry shook his head no. "They're graveyards. If you never get out, you'll walk around forever not knowing that you've never been anything but dead this whole time. And you're getting out if it kills me, my beautiful boy."

"Yes, Mother," he said, and Emma Baron slapped him with her bare hand so hard light flashed behind his eyes and he couldn't close his jaw all the way when he said, "Yes, *Muth-uh.*"

With that, she yawned, stretching her arms out wide, over-performing every little movement, and went off to bed. Blanketless, still wearing his clothes and shoes, Henry laid down on the pallet next to his sisters' bed and closed his eyes for a few moments before it was time to wake them for school.

After school, the other girls ran ahead and Henry held nine-year-old Mixie's hand as they slowly made their way down Forge. Along the way, she asked him why their mother loved him so much more than them.

When he was young, Henry had to figure a lot out for himself. How to cook. Sew. That stuffing newspaper in his shoes kept his feet warm in the winter. When his sisters were born, he swore to always have answers to their questions. The one who took him up on that the most was Mixie. Her daily questions—"Why can I see my breath when it's cold?" "How many people are there?"—kept him on his toes and in the school library during lunch. But there was no answer to what she just asked.

"Why do you think that?"

"I want to see beautiful places." She coughed and wiped her nose on her coat sleeve. Her sinuses gave her trouble every spring, especially in the cold, early weeks. Mixie showed him her mucusy sleeve. "She'd hit you with a ruler if you did that."

"If Mother loved me more, she'd let me sleep," he said and kissed the top of her head.

They walked on, silently, past the two-story storefronts. Past the new filling station. "She makes you talk funny," she finally said. "You talk that way sometimes when Mama's not making you."

Henry didn't know that. He knew his mother wasn't right. And he knew the more she focused what was wrong with her on him, the less she'd focus it on his sisters. But at what cost, he wondered for the first time. To him. To them.

"It's because I need more help than you girls. She says all the time that the four of you are her little princesses."

They stopped walking when their home came into view. Off to the left was the city, with its sturdy, looming buildings they only knew from far away. To the right, the valley, clustered with homes and families they knew instinctively were nothing like theirs. Splitting the view down the center was their block—a row of homes rotting from the inside out like their own teeth.

"I don't believe you," she said.

John Baron was home long enough to brush his wool uniform and be accused of infecting the laundry with "barmaid diseases" by his wife, but neither parent could muster the energy to fight like they meant it if one of them had somewhere to be. As soon as he left, Emma Baron became her other self, gliding slowly around the house, her arms outstretched as though she were feeling the tips of waist-high grass.

Henry made dinner and helped his sisters with their schoolwork until his mother was "off to pray for their little souls."

That night, he sat at the table after the girls fell asleep and willed himself to stay awake, but after nearly three days without sleep, the odds were against him. He rested his head on his arms and told himself he'd be all right so long as he kept his eyes open.

When he woke, his mother was back, sitting with him at the table, her skin lit red by the dying embers of the stove. Her pupils—wide, black yolks—stared blankly ahead, fixed on the far wall. Flat on the table between mother and son sat, instead of a ruler, a carving knife.

"Mother. I'm sorry."

"Have you ever been inside a hospital?" She had to know that he had not. "Rooms full of beds," she went on. "And in every bed, a bony little body full of disease. Sweating, writhing in pain, coughing their disease into the air." She looked at Henry. "And I'm alone, you see. Tending to them the best I can. Wiping their foreheads. Bringing them water they can't drink. But there is no easing their pain. Just agony until, finally, thankfully."

Here, Emma Baron uncrumpled a white handkerchief from her fist and draped it over her face like a veil. Though covered, Henry could feel his mother's eyes on him. "But they lived, right?" he said to the faceless face. "A man on a horse brought you the medicine in time or—"

"They died." She pulled away the white cloth. "They all died."

Henry was about to speak when she sprung on him, covering his mouth with her hand. "Listen," she said.

Just beneath the occasional *pop* of the fire, Mixie's congested breathing was low and rhythmic. His mother took her hand away and pressed it to her chest. "It's here. All the dirt and filth and disease we breathe. It builds up right here like a stopped up drain. A wet lump of black meat that seeps into your veins and lungs."

She didn't speak for a long time. After a show, she was always someone else, somewhere else, and he was somehow a link between her two worlds. Swashbuckling adventures and love stories made sense to the beautiful girl she must have been once, or thought she was, or hoped she was. It was easier for him to be an unwitting accomplice in her delusion than to make things harder than they already were.

But a movie about a lonely nurse gallantly caring for the doomed. She'd never described a movie like that. It must have been like looking out a window, expecting to see the only good thing in your life, and instead of a window, it's a mirror. Looking back is a woman with lines in her face, five children, a drunkard husband, and chapped, leathered hands draped over the water-bleached handle of a dull knife.

But all that was something Henry could only vaguely understand at the time. Except for the knife. He understood that.

"My beautiful boy," she finally said, still staring at her sleeping daughters. "Do you know what the cruelest thing on earth is?" Henry had no guess. "When a long life is a slow death."

She scooted her chair back and walked heavy-footed to the bedroom, closing the door behind her. No lesson tonight, Henry curled up on his pallet.

This version of his mother was new. In a good or bad way—and this was, of course, very bad—it was rare that his mother gave her daughters any thought at all. What was much more common was an idea occurring to Emma Baron and instantly becoming the most important idea she's ever heard right before some other idea came along to take its place.

Which is exactly what would happen tomorrow, he told himself, staring at the ceiling, listening to his sisters' breathing. His lessons would resume tomorrow and tomorrow will be just like every other day.

"*Wund-a-full*," he practiced in a hissing whisper. "I *cahnt*. I *cahn*. *Thahnk* you, *Muth-uh*. *Thahnk* you. *Thahnk* you. I will be with you *for-evah*."

Henry awoke the next morning to daylight and laughter. To his sisters sitting at the table and the smells of cooking breakfast. His mother was frying eggs and slicing ham steak with the carving knife. The girls saw him stirring and waved, barely able to contain themselves.

"Henry! Henry! Breakfast!"

He couldn't remember the last time he'd eaten breakfast or saw his mother up and moving before school. She smiled at him. And not her airy, titled-head, eyes-almost-closed smile that made Henry wonder if she knew who or where she was. Standing over the stove, setting ham steaks on the griddle, she was a picture of a mother. Like how he imagined every other mother was every morning.

Things weren't back to normal. They were something better.

All day at school, rested and full, he felt something akin to what his mother felt after a night at the movies. Like someone else living some other life. Though he held little hope that the mother who sent them off to school would be the one who greeted them when they arrived home, his sisters devouring the morning's attention was a memory he would always cherish.

But he was wrong again. She was neither the woman from the night before nor was she the doe-eyed lady-in-waiting. Just a mother happy to see all five of her children. She kissed each on the cheek and ushered them inside. Their father was who knew where, so there was no shouting, heavy tension, or wild accusations. But with the way things were going, maybe even him being home would have been all right.

She spent the day cleaning the girls' bedding and nightclothes. They hung damp from a line stretching behind the front door to the far side of the room. After the girls wore themselves out running around and through the hanging laundry, Emma Baron lined them side-by-side on their bed for inspection. "When was the last time you urchins were washed?" she said with only a hint of put-on accent. "You're going to start growing vegetables behind your ears." She hid a carrot in her sleeve, pretended to pull it from Georgia's hair, and the girls howled with laughter.

For hours, the setting sun casting the room in warm reds and golds, their mother heated water from the sink pump and refilled the washtub. Dipping the girls in the water one at a time, she called them her "little chickens" and smothered their wet heads and cheeks with kisses. During her turn in the washtub, Mixie smiled with all her teeth at Henry. Because he had not lied. Right then, and maybe from now on, she was her mother's little princess.

The room smelling of Ivory soap and rosewater instead of Kerosene oil and damp wood, Henry took down the laundry, remade the girls' bed, and set out their suddenly chalk-white nightgowns. Emma Baron cooked dinner— fried fish and hominy—and all six of them ate packed in together at the table. She tucked the girls into bed, read them a story, and kissed them goodnight.

Once they were asleep, she put on her hat and coat and stood over Henry who was still seated at the table. "Do you think they had a nice day?" she whispered.

"I don't think they've ever had a nicer day."

"That's exactly the day I wanted them to have." Henry looked up at his mother. She was looking at her daughters, a gentle smile on her face. "I'm going out, Henry," she went on. "Go to sleep. No lessons tonight."

After she left, Henry washed and dried the dishes. The only decoration on any of the walls was a framed portrait of his mother as a teenager. She had been beautiful. That was true. Henry thought about how when you're beautiful and young, maybe the world leads you to believe that your life is going to turn out different than what's really in store for you. Not his sisters, though. They were beautiful and young, but other than what little Henry could do for them, life had not shown them enough good to make them think they were entitled to any. They had no inkling that they deserved more or that more was even possible.

But maybe his sisters' lives could be different if they had a mother who taught them what it is to dream. And if that were to happen, maybe a few of those dreams might actually come true. Henry tossed some planks into the stove, blew out the lights, left one lamp burning, and stretched out on his pallet, hoping that was the mother they now had. Which had been the only dream he ever allowed himself to have.

He would be grateful for the rest of his life that he didn't know what sound finally woke him, but what followed would be branded into his brain forever. Henry opened his eyes to Mixie huddled underneath the table, looking small and wild-eyed, her knees pressed to her chest. In his half-sleep, Henry thought he was having a nightmare—that the bed up above him had turned alive, a wooden throat convulsing on a bone. He stood, looked at the bed, and saw something even more incomprehensible.

The bedding and nightclothes that had been so white, so new and clean-looking when the evening began, were dark and wet with blood. Straddling Eula, Mary, and Georgia—though he could not make the three girls out individually—was his mother, drenched also in the wet darkness, plunging the carving knife deep into the twining of arms, legs, and golden hair.

"Shhhhh," Emma Baron said to the girls, her face calm and deliberate. "Shhhhh."

Henry tugged Mixie out from under the table and dragged her towards the door. The movement distracted their mother from her work. She jumped off the bed and took hold of Mixie's other arm. Mixie screamed.

"Henry," said his mother. "They're sick. You don't understand."

Son and mother wrenched the girl back forth. Henry stretched into a T, Mixie's wrist was slipping from his hand as he grasped for the doorknob. "I'm helping them," she said and slashed at Henry with the knife, slicing his shoulder, the metal gnashing against bone.

His arm went limp. Mixie slipped from his weakened grip and was jerked into her mother's blood-soaked clothes. The last thing he saw before opening the door and running into the black night toward the nearest lit building was Emma Baron wrapping her arms around Mixie. Enveloping her. Gone.

It was still dark. Henry sat alone in the small parcel of muddy grass that was their front yard. His arm was sticky with old and new blood. John Baron, drunk, his collar undone at the neck, sat on an upturned milk crate. He was blubbering, surrounded by five or six more policemen, hands buried in their pockets or patting Henry's father on the back.

None of the adults tended to Henry. They didn't seem to notice him there. He barely noticed himself. Or much else. The reverberating pain in his shoulder. The misting rain so thin it barely made anything wet. The cold. The thin ribbon of white mist coiling away from his wound and into the air.

He lived for his sisters. And to protect his mother from what the neighborhood might say if they knew the truth about her. Now, every purpose he had on earth was being carried out of his home by men, one at a time. Five shapes tucked into red-blotted sheets.

His mother always told him that one day he would see such beautiful places. He never believed her. That he would see them. That they even existed. At least not how they existed in her mind. He would have settled for Georgia,

Eula, Mary, and Mixie having just the slightest chance at life, even if he had to trade his own in the bargain.

Alone, sitting in mud and blood, numbed to his core, he finally believed her. There had to be those beautiful, magical places in this world because there were places that weren't this place. That's what she'd meant this whole time. To get there, all he had to do was stand up and walk. It didn't matter in which direction because every direction led away from this cold, dead place. East would take him past the movie house. South would take him through the city. North, through the valley. West was just a wall of darkness, but even that was somewhere else.

Stand. Walk. That's all Henry had to do. Walk until nothing anywhere was something he could see right now and then keep going. The rain would cleanse him. The wind would carry him. He would eat when there was food. He would make a bed of the grass or stone beneath his feet when tired. And when he woke, stand up—walk. And never stop. And never stop.

"*Wund-a-full,*" he mouthed, lost inside this gift of a dream. "*Wund-a-full. Wund-a-full. Wund-a-full.*"

ACKNOWLEDGMENTS

I probably should have quit all this a long time ago and become a dentist. In recognition of the absurd chain of events that prevented that from happening, I offer the following heartfelt thanks and gratitude:

To The Ohio State University and the University of Mississippi, in particular their English Departments, in particular the patience, wisdom, and mentorship of Michelle Herman, Lee K. Abbott, Tom Franklin, David Galef, and Barry Hannah (rest in peace). To Cup O Joe Lennox in Columbus, Ohio (circa 2002 through 2006), and Uptown Coffee in Oxford, Mississippi (circa 2006 through 2009)—the closest I've ever come to having an office. Cup O Joe Lennox no longer exits, but still. To Lori Ostlund, obviously. To Anneabel Gemmel for making the most beautiful book cover I have ever seen. To David Bowen and all of the good people at New American Press. To New American Press's impeccable taste in books and judges. To the *Green Mountains Review*, *Blood Orange Review*, *Ampersand*, *Brink Magazine*, *Digital America Magazine*, *is this up*, *Water~Stone*, and *Harvard Review* for giving these stories their first life. Some of these places don't exist anymore, but still. To the indomitable city of Barberton, Ohio. To Hudson, Ohio, the jewel of my heart. To the Rubber City. To my copilots, Ryan Bubalo, Teresa Petro, and Karin Davidson. To a vast battalion of invaluable friends and intimidatingly talented peers. To my little squad of a family. To my CO, Emilia Kandl.

And last but not least, I wish to thank spite.

Without you, all of you—and so many others—this book wouldn't be. And I'd be a dead-hearted dentist. Thank you.

SETH BORGEN's first collection of stories, *If I Die in Ohio*, received the New American Fiction Prize. His work has appeared in *Water~Stone*, *Green Mountains Review*, *Harvard Review*, and elsewhere. He received his MFA from the University of Mississippi. Seth teaches creative writing and writes full-time. He lives in Akron, Ohio.